Beautiful Notes

SIERRA ZINKE

to sharon, my grandmother, thank you. there is not a day that goes by that I don't miss you.

Playlist

This playlist is the perfect soundtrack as you dive into *Beautiful Notes*, setting the mood for every twist, turn, and tender moment.

Some of my favorites included are:

Pink Skies | Zach Bryan

Orchestra | Drew Ryn

Thought You Should Know | Morgan Wallen

Love You Tonight | Ella Langley

I Hate That It's True | Dean Lewis

I Can Do It With A Broken Heart | Taylor Swift

Wait! | Kelsea Ballerini

Prologue: 10 years ago, Milwaukee

OLIVIA

Of course it's raining in Milwaukee as our plane lands. I take my headphones off, to settle the anxiety of missing any landing announcements, only to be bombarded with the sound of the cold rain pinging off the metal plane. The sound is the type that would lead you to curl up on the couch, with a fuzzy blanket, a glass of wine and a good book. It's not uncommon for it to rain in October here, but after yesterday, the last thing I want is more dreary sadness in my life.

My friends Mason, Carolina, and Savannah are all sitting at my house waiting for my Uber to pull up. I haven't even told them the extent of what happened, just that I was getting on a flight and coming back to Milwaukee. Two days early.

Mason: I got chocolate ice cream.

Savannah: I got us some extra wine & gin for you.

Caroline: Amazon cart is full of rope, duct tape, and a human-size garbage bag.

Our group chat continues to ping as I climb into my Uber for the long ride home back to the house. I keep my head down, hood up, to hide my tear streaked, puffy eyes. I just want to sit in silence. Looking out the window, mentally prepare for the tsunami of tears and emotions about to hit when I walk in that front door.

My friends are the most kind-hearted, loving, have-your-back type of friends. Which means I will be bombarded with hugs, and I will definitely cry. It's going to be a messy, ugly cry. Almost like the rain drops racing down the car window.

In early October, Milwaukee is generally sixty degrees, with a healthy mix of sun and rain, except today. Today, it's barely fifty degrees and raining, and I would like nothing more than to disappear into my bed forever.

My phone starts vibrating with a call and I pull it out of my pocket to see who it is. Noah's name rolls across my phone and a photo of the two of us from high school graduation fills the entire screen. Oh, fuck no. I immediately hit reject on the call. There is not a chance in hell I'm answering that. I would rather be thrown off the ski mountain and crash through the trees before I talk to him again.

Noah: Ollie, answer the phone

If I wasn't in the Uber, I would likely throw my phone into my bedroom and pretend it's lost. My phone starts ringing. Noah. *Again.* Deny.

Noah: Ollie, please.

The Uber rounds the corner to my house, and I can see my friends standing in the big picture window that overlooks my living room waiting for my arrival. I don't know how I got so fortunate to have these amazing people ready to go to war for me without even knowing the situation, but I also know I'm not getting out of this conversation easily after coming home two days early from the trip that was supposed to change my entire life.

I've completed the first half of my first semester as a freshman at Marquette, where I met the three amazing friends, all standing in my living room, waiting for me to get home. We are planning to move in together in the fall when our respective leases are up and I truly am so lucky to have them. Milwaukee is my new home, I try to tell myself, only half convinced I'll be able to make a forever life for myself here.

Anything is better than being back home in the middle of nowhere, going back to a life where our families are close and I have to relive this pain everyday. Plus what am I going to tell our families? He has the luxury of not going home ever and I have to be the one to tell them everything.

Especially Cole. Oh god...Cole. What am I going to tell him? I shake my head trying to remove the thought and the feeling of panic the thought stirs up. That is a problem for another day.

My life might be falling apart now, but it won't be forever because Milwaukee is where I want to be. Not Noah's arms.

Or at least I'm going to keep telling myself that until it becomes my reality.

I don't even make it up the seven brick steps into my townhouse before the silent tears start streaming. I only make it another four steps through the front door before I am tackled by Gus, golden fur flying all over my face as his paws sit on my shoulders and he starts licking my face, salty tears and all.

I round the corner of the hallway into the open living room to everyone staring at the doorway waiting for me. All it takes is one look at them, the sadness and sympathy written across their faces, for me to break down all over again.

"Oh, honey," Caroline says as she wraps her arms around me. I bury my face into her shoulder as Savannah comes over rubbing my back and pulling my rain drenched hair out of my face and mouth.

I feel a gentle tap on my shoulder and they gesture to the couch already equipped with every throw pillow in the house and my favorite green blanket ready for me. They not only came to my house, but set everything up to optimize my comfort without even knowing what happened. How did I get so lucky?

I see Mason walking back into the living room from the kitchen carrying a small wooden tray with three different cups on it. He gently sets it on the coffee table in front of me, moving at a snail's pace to avoid spilling anything. I realize there are three different cups with three different beverages in it, a bright yellow mug with tea, a small square glass with a clear liquid and a lime on the side, and a stemless wine glass with a hefty pour of white wine.

"I didn't know what you'd want, so I brought you all three," he says, placing a hand on my shoulder before sitting on the other side of Savannah next to me.

"Thank you," I reply with a soft smile and a sniffle as I pick up the clear drink discovering it's gin and downing half of it before I begin telling them about Oklahoma. At least as much as I'm willing to share.

♪ ♪ ♪

I don't remember when I retrieved the letter, the last letter that Noah wrote to me while in basic training. I don't remember what prompted Caroline and Mason to antagonize me to throw it away, rip it up, burn it, and cleanse it from my life. But I did grab the box of letters, I did grab the last one, and I did rip it into shreds.

Maybe it was the wine, maybe it was twelve missed calls and text messages from Noah before Caroline hid my phone, or maybe it was the wave of emotions, the anger, the sadness, or even the confusion.

Chapter 1: Present Day

OLIVIA

"C'mon, Olivia!" I hear Caroline yell over the stereo that's playing "Any Man of Mine" by Shania Twain.

"Ugh," I groan to myself as I dig through my closet for my go-to bar outfit. Faux leather pants and a dark red top that accentuates me in all the right ways.

It's been Caroline and Mason's mission for the last ten years to help me get over Noah. Take Olivia out to the bars, wing woman her into some nice man's arms, and let the rest be history. If only it were that easy.

Don't get me wrong, I have been in other relationships over the years but nothing's ever felt right. I typically let things fizzle out after a few months because there is no point in wasting anyone else's time or effort if it isn't going to work out in the long run. I'm perfectly happy with the random hookup here and there.

Mason and Savannah finally admitted they were into each other and have been together for almost two years now, and I think Mason is planning to propose in the springtime. Caroline and Ben have been together for six months and things are getting serious between them.

I love my friends and I know they mean well, but I really don't need to be in a relationship. I have my job, running, and plans for my future. I'm making a difference in people's lives and I want to expand that to as many people in Wisconsin as possible. I was just asked to present at a school regarding physical therapy and the different facets of it. Definitely no time for a boyfriend.

"Coming! Just curling my hair," I yell back as I frantically try to pull myself together as quickly as possible. I don't particularly want to go to the bar tonight but also don't want to disappoint Caroline. She's been the best rock of a friend I could ever asked for.

The Pub Down the Street is literally a small pub down the street. It's a super small bar that is family-friendly, with outdoor seating during the day, but at 10 p.m. the entire atmosphere shifts into more of a club. The tables in the center of the space are moved to make room for a dance floor with booths and bench seating around the outside. We typically claim a round booth in the corner and walk up to the bar, where our favorite bartender, Felix, makes us cocktails. He knows the group rules and fits in with us like a glove. Felix has been working at The Pub for as long as I can remember. He's so good at his job that he can even predict the drinks we want simply by our moods when we arrive.

In anticipation of it being exceptionally busy, since it is Friday, we leave the house early enough that it's not quite pitch black outside, where you can't see and it takes forever to adjust, but dark enough that street lights are on and the warm lights from businesses and townhouses illuminate the path.

The sidewalk is lined with crisp gray-brown snow that has melted and refroze a dozen times when the sun warms the street and then drops into sub-zero temperatures at night, making the sidewalk slick in some damp areas and a potential hazard for the clumsy friends. It is me. I'm the clumsy friend. It never fails I fall at least once a year and bruise my ego and pride walking home from the bar after a few too many.

Fortunately, the Pub Down the Street is close and the three block walk, or trudge, as we call it, when the wind blows through the streets creates a wind tunnel that not even our down jackets can warm us.

Caroline and I typically walk arm in arm to and from the bar, acting out the unspoken girl code rules that no girl is left behind. More recently Ben has taken that place and wants to walk her down the street for "safety." As if she is any less safe walking with me. It's not like we aren't all together. Truthfully, I feel like Ben has become a little clingy lately, and I can tell that it's annoying Caroline by the way she rolls her eyes as he slides next to her pulling her close.

We bop down the street, ready for a night full of music and dancing together, when the green awning, with beautiful icicle Christmas lights hanging from it come into view. The smell of french fries waft into the air as people open the door. We quicken our pace in anticipation and excitement to see what Felix makes for each of us.

In a not-so-shocking turn of events, Felix reads each of us perfectly. Handing Caroline an espresso martini for her first drink knowing she needs a boost of caffeine after an incredibly hard story today. A fatal accident regarding a child, that she was responsible for covering the vast majority of the day. Those stories are always the hardest and the most draining mentally and physically. A soft smile slides across her wind blown face when he hands her the martini, a silent thank you for always getting it right.

Today, Felix gives me something different than my usual and I cannot help but wonder what he is seeing in me today that is different.

He hands me a short glass with a light green cocktail that smells spicy. I give him a confused look and he responds with "You look spicy today, let's give you a drink that matches."

I feel a warmth come over my cheeks unsure how to respond, but a little embarrassed at the same time.

"Relax, Liv," he continues, "It's a cucumber jalapeno margarita, your shoulders are sitting up by your ears and you're standing as rigid as a two by four. You need a drink to get you all loosey goosey and on the dance floor."

I'm instantly floored that he takes the time to notice all of those little factoids about us when he is the only bartender and there are probably fifteen other patrons waiting.

We sit at our usual small round booth in the back of the bar. It's dimly lit and the music is thirty octaves too loud but gives us a place to lay claim when our feet start to hurt and we need a break from the dance floor. Plus it's far enough away from everyone else that we don't worry about leaving anything at the table throughout the night.

I'm getting settled at the booth with Caroline while Felix finishes everyone's drinks when a deep, bone chilling draft of cold air fills the bar, when two guys walk in the front door, flinging it open as wide as it can go.

"No, Caroline," I say sternly before she even gets a word out. Her big brown eyes shrink, and the glow of excitement fades into disappointment at my immediate rejection.

"Come on, Olivia," she exclaims clearly annoyed. "When was the last time you got laid? You have needs. Needs that running can't fix. Plus, look at this man."

The man is attractive, tall and athletically built, with thighs that could shatter a watermelon. Don't even get me started on his biceps, holy heck. His blond hair is short, and his brown eyes remind me of the espresso martini Felix just made.

"I don't need anyone to fill my needs, that's what Vlad is for," I reply calmly. Vlad, the blue vibrator, lives in the comfort of my nightstand and is amazing at his job.

"Vlad is great but when was the last time you were with someone? And I mean someone who you actually had a connection with?" Caroline replies hastily.

Noah. Noah was the last time I felt truly connected to someone, and the fact that after ten years he still has this much of an effect on me makes me angry.

I returned from Oklahoma and instantly threw myself into school, work, and my friendships, promising to never get that close to someone again especially when all they do is leave.

"I don't need to connect with someone, Caroline. I'm happy with my solo lifestyle," I reply, and she frowns at me.

"You can't hate all men, forever. It's not healthy," she bursts out before walking out onto the dance floor with Mason, Savannah, and Ben who are eagerly waiting for her.

I feel the simmer of annoyance bubbling in my abdomen knowing that she is right, but there is one man I don't hate. I can't bring myself to hate him no matter how hard I try. He constantly lives in the back of my mind and is often poking his way through the barrier into the forefront of my mind.

No matter who I talk to or who I date, whether we have everything in common or absolutely nothing in common, I find myself drifting back to *him*. And it's fucking irritating, so I've sworn off dating all together.

I hear something ding, but being in a crowded room I just assume it's someone else's phone.

Ding. Ding. Ding.

The text sound continues to alert me of incoming texts, and although we have a no phone at the bar rule, everyone is distracted with dancing so I pull it out to make sure everything is okay.

Noah: Hey

Cole: so I ran into Noah...

Cole: I'm sorry.

Noah: I heard you're coming home in two weeks, let's get drinks and catch up? I miss you, Ollie.

My heart stops in its tracks. Excuse me? Noah Kneland, after ten years of "Happy Birthday" and "Merry Christmas" texts, decides he misses me? What do I even say back to that? I miss you? Gross. No. Do I miss him? Probably. Am I going to tell him that? Absolutely not.

"Phone!" I hear Mason yell from the other end of the dance floor as I'm being rushed by my entire group of friends. I have never been so happy to buy a round of shots if it means my phone gets taken and hidden until the night is over.

Why would Noah say that? We haven't seen each other in ten years and never once has he expressed missing me.

I fake the biggest smile I can as I hand my phone to Caroline, to keep from breaking the rules when it dings a fifth time.

Noah again. All she has to do is look at the screen to know we need more tequila. And a lot of it.

Chapter 2

OLIVIA

I wake up with a raging headache and very little recollection after the third shot of tequila and dancing. I roll over in bed and my entire body is aching from my head down to my toes. I can only assume that after the third shot, there were more, many more.

I smell cinnamon buns from the kitchen, and know that something happened when I remember why we were taking shots in the first place.

My phone. Where is my phone? Usually, it gets set on the wireless charger on top of the nightstand. Flying out of bed, I get a wave of the spins as I find my comfiest black slippers. Looking in the mirror to analyze what state my face and hair are in, I'm impressed that I remembered to take my makeup off, but chuckle at the mop I have on top of my head and the ratty oversized t-shirt I'm wearing. Did I try to braid it and give up, throwing it into a bun? Did I try to run a marathon in my sleep? Where did this shirt even come from? Another set of spins have me clutching the dresser to right myself.

Who the hell let me drink that much tequila last night? I blame Felix. If I had just started and stuck with gin the world wouldn't be upside down right now.

Opening my bedroom door, the smell of breakfast intensifies cinnamon buns, bacon, coffee steaming. Someone died. There's no other explanation for my favorite, comfort, breakfast food to be ready for me after a night out.

"What's going on? Who died?" I ask lightheartedly when walking into the kitchen where everyone is. "We only have cinnamon buns when there's a crisis or it's exam week. And considering we all graduated years ago, there must be a crisis."

They all stare at me in silence for what feels like an eternity. Clearly, I'm the one everyone expects to be a hot mess this morning.

"Do you remember anything from last night?" Savannah asks.

"Yes," I reply "as long as it was before the tequila" I finish under my breath hoping that they don't hear me. "Have any of you seen my phone? It didn't make it into my room with me last night."

Radio silence.

"Okay, guys, look, I'm fine. Yes, I know that Noah texted me. Yes, I remember he asked to catch up when I'm home. But, no, I'm not going to go, and no, I'm not going to get moody and shut down all day," I say, getting slightly annoyed.

Caroline and Mason share a look that says they have been scheming, and that is never a good thing. Mason nods, placing an arm around Savannah. Ben steps around Caroline as if shielding her from the bomb that is about to be dropped.

"We think you should meet with Noah," Caroline says, sliding a taped-together piece of scrap paper onto the counter.

Now it's my turn for radio silence. 'Cause there is not a single chance I've heard that correctly. Everything around me feels fuzzy like I'm underwater.

"Olivia, we know that you will always love Noah. He's always been a huge part of your life and you haven't been able to get over everything that happened in Oklahoma. Liv, we saved this for you..." Caroline slides the paper closer to me. Mason drops his arm off Savannah's shoulder sliding around the table as I stare down at the tattered piece of paper in front of me.

The letter. The letter I ripped up nearly ten years ago, all the pieces taped together to form one sheet of paper again. I have the sudden urge to vomit and run away, run away from everyone around me and live under a rock. Caroline walks around the opposite side of the counter, enclosing me into Mason. She gently slides the letter off the counter into my hands as they tremble and my eyes water. I don't even realize we shuffle across the room from the kitchen island into the living room until we settle into the corner of the couch. I take a throw pillow into my lap to clutch as they take up the seats next to me.

"Where did you get this?" I ask, my words trembling off my lips.

"I know we pressured you to rip it up and write Noah off...but after everything that night, I thought you may want this one day. Reread it, Liv," She's only ever called me Liv when she's sorry or wants to show her support and love for me. "Reread it, think about what you want. If you want this to truly be over or if you want to hear him out and maybe even forgive him. But you should meet with him," she finishes.

I'm speechless after hearing what Caroline has to say, and I can tell that this wasn't easy for them because they're all huddled together around the far corner of the island in solidarity with one another. Mason's head is bowed and he is looking at the faux granite countertop. He hates hurting people and I know they are worried about my feelings.

Caroline is right. I have, and likely always will have, a place in my heart for Noah. But it's not fair to either of us to continue on this way. I don't think I'm mentally prepared to see him, though. Going home is going to be hard enough, having been only six months since my grandmother, my best friend, passed away. And now I'm supposed to go home for the holidays like everything is normal and "catch up" with Noah.

The thought is overwhelming and I'm starting to feel like I'm underwater again. I'm grateful to have friends who care enough about me to do the difficult things, have the difficult conversations with me, and support me through whatever I decide to do.

"Okay," I whisper finally. "Okay, I will think about it," I finish, sounding genuine.

I consider texting Noah back immediately before I chicken out and pretend it never happened.

The sparkle that emerges in Mason's eyes, paired with that big relieved smile, melts my heart. I know what I have to do, but also those cinnamon buns smell too good to sit on the platter staring at me any longer.

"Okay, so, can we eat now?" I ask and before the sentence is finished the silence is replaced by laughter as we head into the kitchen for breakfast.

♪ ♪ ♪

Ollie,

Things have been crazy here at basic, we get up between 0300 and 0500 and have some training all day long. To think it has been eight weeks already is insane. This phase is all about weapons training, convoy operations, and military operations.

I can't believe I graduate in two weeks, but I would be lying to you if I said this has been easy, I am not talking about physically either. I can do all the activities but it gets lonely not being able to communicate with my people. We started with 84 recruits in my class and this week we only have 46 left. I was fortunate to be able to call Mom and Bec the other day for a check-in, especially about Archie. Everything is good and they are so excited to come to Oklahoma for graduation. I wish I was able to have more time to talk to you aside from letters.

I miss you, Ollie. I know we left things at a weird place when I left for training but if this journey has taught me anything, home is with you, Ollie. Thank you for being my support system and my best friend. I have to go we are getting ready for the final event of the day but if you get anything out of this letter, I want you to know,

I'm in love with you, Olivia.

~N

My eyes instantly well up with tears as I finish reading the letter for the third time today. This time, hiding in the comfort of my room, wrapped in my favorite dark green blanket seeking any comfort. This letter was my entire life ten years ago, and now sitting here at my desk, I don't know how to feel.

I was so certain of every aspect of my life, I was in love with my best friend, I was going to be a kick-ass physical therapist, and I would travel wherever I needed to be to have a family with Noah. Well, at least one of those things came true. I didn't care about having friends, a support system, or being close to my family. Hell, Noah was my family and all I wanted was to be with him. I didn't even bother writing him back after this final letter, I was going to surprise him at graduation. Show up at graduation with his family, and tell him that I was in love with him too. That I was excited for our adventure and our life together.

Gosh, how could I have been so naive and stupid? That is not how the world works, and he flipped that plan upside down in just a matter of minutes. I almost let one person completely unravel my life. But if one good thing came out of this, it's that I achieved my dreams. I'm a kick-ass physical therapist in one of the most beautiful cities in the United States, with the most amazing friends who are my family and will be here at the drop of a hat, if necessary.

You don't have to forgive and forget, Olivia. It's okay to forgive and remember the bad. But never forget that we never know the full extent of someone else's actions, what drives them to make their decisions, or what they are going through outside of their life with you and it's not fair to hold that against them.

I remember my grandmother's words like a punch to the gut and know instantly what I have to do. I pull my phone off my desk charger and text Noah.

Me: I'm driving back on December 22nd, we can plan something then.

Chapter 3

OLIVIA

The two weeks leading up to my trip back to Fisher Creek flies by. Between work and getting ready for the holidays I don't have time to overthink or even really consider meeting up with Noah until I'm in Fisher Creek. I only last a whole twelve hours before I'm itching to get out of the house and escape my mind.

The cold, brisk air hits my face as I brush my hair out of my eyes. I'm walking to start my old car to venture to the only coffee shop within a twenty-mile radius. I feel the subtle vibrations of my phone ringing in my heavy-padded pocket, and as I pull it out I see Mason's name on the screen.

"Enjoying the cold?" He chuckles as I answer the phone.

"Jerk…" But he's right, I really hate the cold and am honestly a little jealous that he traveled back to Southern California while I traveled to my hometown for the holiday. My hometown, Fisher Creek, is the epitome of a small town and there is a reason most of our graduating class left without looking back. I fully intended on being one of them like my sister, Penelope, but things changed. This is the first holiday season without my beloved grandmother and all I want is to spend it with my family and a bottle of wine.

"It's eighteen degrees, not including the wind, and I'm not even caffeinated yet," I grumble, starting the car and blasting the heat.

"You're a grump this morning. I was just curious if you finally said yes to hanging out with Noah tonight?"

My entire body tenses at the sound of Noah's name and the fact that he asked to get drinks while I'm home. We were inseparable in high school, the best of friends, until, well, we just weren't.

But time does that to people, right? They move to different cities, take different life paths, and just grow apart.

"I don't know. I only get to see the boys for a few days a year, I should probably just stay in with the family," I blurt out as quickly as possible, trying to avoid thinking too much about the topic. Everyone who knows Noah and me knows that I have such a soft spot for this man even after all these years, even after everything that happened.

"Stop being a chicken, your family is going to go to bed at eight p.m, and then you're going to be bored. Go out! Plus, you never know what might happen," he says, and I can hear the smirk on his face as he says that last bit. Living with Mason means he is fully aware of my love life and all of its crazy ups and downs.

"Goodbye, Mason, I'm going to get coffee now," I say as I hang up the phone before he can badger me anymore regarding my relationship status.

Mason and I have been friends since we both moved to Milwaukee for PT school. He moved out of Southern California to experience something different. He wanted to see the snow and cold, and for whatever reason was a big Bucks fan. I moved to Milwaukee to move off the farm but stay close enough to go home if necessary. Little did we know, we moved into the same neighborhood, and were in all of the same introduction classes at school. That first day, I walked into the large 150-person lecture hall and just stopped. I have always been relatively reserved, and never really flourished in big crowds. And then, there I was in a new city, a new school, knowing no one aside from some faces I recognized from the required class Facebook page.

Mason walked in behind me, stopped next to me, smiled, and said, "Come on, let's go sit." Then ushered me toward the middle of the big hall before I could nod in agreement. We have been friends since that day ten years ago, living together for the last nine of them.

I hear the ridiculous quacking text tone of my group chat with Mason, Caroline and Savannah, reminding me to silence my phone before getting to the coffee shop. Even ten years later, I'm still baffled that I haven't changed the tone yet. When we first started the group chat to plan nights out and keep track of everyone it was a quiet little chat only used when necessary but the closer we became as friends the louder the chat got. I frequently ignored the chat on the premise that it was just a text notification like any other text I got. Until Caroline had my phone one night and changed the ringtone to the most annoying duck noise she could find in the phone setting under the premise that I would never ignore a text that reminded me of home. She then proceeded to leave the ringer on and tell everyone to avoid the group chat until the next morning when they blew it up while I was contemplating my night choices. And yet after all these years and jokes later, I never changed it.

I ignore the text as I pull up to the local coffee shop, Creek and Kettle. After parking, crossing the snowy street, and ordering my decadent hot peppermint mocha, I sit down at a little wooden table and look around amazed at how timeless our community is.

Julianna, the owner, played on my high school soccer team and went on to get a degree in business administration before returning to our hometown to open up this coffee shop. The building was a breakfast restaurant until the owner passed away and there was no family to take over the business.

When Julianna bought it, she kept everything. And I mean literally everything, the old tables, booths, bar stools, everything. The only difference is that she refurbished it all so they have the old-timey look and feel, but, functionally, are brand new. She maintained the brick interior wall and turned it into a beautiful accent piece to draw attention to the large picture windows in the front.

I look up from my small table and can remember back to being a child and having breakfast here with my grandparents, looking at the same beautiful Christmas decorations that I see now.

If there is one thing this small town does well, it's Christmas. Nothing changes year after year but it never fails that I'm always mesmerized by the beauty and dedication everyone has to the holidays and traditions.

Pulling out my phone, I see that the text isn't from the group chat, but from him. And I'm instantly transported back in time.

Chapter 4

NOAH

Being home after so many years is always weird. The steadiness of the house, the clean air, the smell of the lake with every step outside, and the snow. The biggest thing that gets to me about being home is the constant thoughts of Olivia. It's been too many years since we have seen each other. Since everything changed.

I'm not the same person I was then. I have witnessed unspeakable things and have traveled across the world...and she is a doctor now. I overheard Cole at the gym telling someone about the volunteer work she does with various Milwaukee organizations. She's a doctor who is coming home for the first time since her grandmother died and is considering seeing me.

"You should see if she wants to get drinks" I hear my sister call from the bathroom as she is getting ready for school this morning.

"I have," I growl back at her.

"Well, try harder, it's the first time you're both back at the same time, and I miss"

I slam the door shut before she can finish that sentence. Even though I know she's right. Bec is almost always right.

Ollie is more than my best friend's sister. She's always been more. She's a part of this family. Bec looks up to her and Ollie takes care of her as if she were her own biological sister. She brings cards and still texts Mom on all important dates and always thinks about my family.

I need to do something, anything. Anything to distract me from the fact that she still has not texted me back. We have always kept in intermittent contact. Text messages on birthdays and holidays but nothing more than niceties and formalities. I want to believe that most of that was due to being in the Army and having deployed overseas time and time again, I can't help but think about what would be different now if I had acted differently on that day all those years ago.

I grab a light jacket, slide on my running shoes, grab Archie's leash, and whistle for my four-legged best friend. Archie comes walloping down the hallway at full speed wiggling with big fluffy ears flapping and tongue sticking out the side of his mouth. He knows what time it is. I may only get to see this big goofy mutt when I'm home on leave, but he is my favorite running partner. We open the front door and set off, one step at a time. The blinding reflection of the sun off the snow causes us to be cautious the first few steps not to slip on any snow or ice.

Running, or exercise in general, has always been the best way for me to clear my mind and avoid shutting down or acting irrationally. I learned this relatively quickly after my dad died and everything went to shit.

My therapist at the time suggested I needed an outlet of some sort, specifically a healthy outlet. Mom's depression was getting worse, and I was an angry high school boy trying to hold everything together while mourning the loss of my father. And there was just one night

I couldn't keep it together anymore. My options were to lose my absolute shit on my kid sister who didn't understand why Mom was still in bed refusing to get up, to eat, or play with her, or to yell at my already broken mother.

I had enough self-control at the moment to know none of those were good options or the right choice, so I left the house. My brain told me the best option was to run away. So I started running down the driveway toward the town. I ran for thirty full minutes before I realized that I wasn't raging anymore.

And I haven't stopped running since.

So here I am, running in December in Wisconsin, trying to run away from the self-deprecating what-ifs as to why Ollie hasn't responded, and hoping she will text me back.

Chapter 5

OLIVIA

I can hardly open the message without feeling a whirl of anxiety hitting me, my knee immediately starts to bounce. I feel like I'm back in high school new, anxious, shy, and sitting at a giant table in the cafeteria.

Sitting at that large table during orientation introduction freshman year. We live on different sides of town, but all went to the same high school based on proximity. They divided us into groups so we are required to mingle and meet new people at the school. Each group has an upper-classman assigned to it to help facilitate discussion. Noah is assigned to my table.

"Great. My brother's best friend. At least it's someone I know," I think to myself. The other part of me is nervous because I've always wanted to be part of Noah and Cole's inner circle, but Noah always shuts it down.

We're sitting across from each other along with five other students and are assigned various tasks and boring icebreaker games. I hate icebreakers, I would much rather keep to myself, nose in a book, or be out on the soccer field running. Noah is chatting with the freshman guy next to him, they're both on the soccer team so they have been acquainted for weeks.

"Just keep to yourself and this session will be over soon," *I think to myself as everyone in my group is laughing at a joke.* "Play along and then you can get ready for practice," *my inner monologue talks to myself through this dreaded moment that is too loud, drowning out the sound of anyone talking to me until I hear.*

"Olivia, it's your turn...Olivia...hey...Ollie?"

I snap back to reality. Noah is sitting across from me, staring at me reading and my name tag, as if he didn't already know my name. I want to roll my eyes, annoyed he is pretending to not know me when I realize he called me Ollie. No one has ever called me Ollie before, it reminds me of a boy's name. But it sounds so natural and feels so right out of his mouth.

"Hi, sorry, I was just thinking. I'm Olivia, and I live in Fisher Creek on the Bennett Family Farm. I play soccer too," *I say, quickly coming back to reality and realizing we're actually participating in this icebreaker game.*

"That is so cool, four of the seven of us play soccer!" *another guy says.*

Noah and I are still looking at each other. The corner of his mouth starts to curl into a smile as he says something about us all practicing together one day.

I have known Noah for as long as I can remember. He and Cole met on the soccer field in kindergarten rec ball and have played together since. But even after all these years of knowing him, I've never really looked at him. Like, really looked at him and soaked in all of his features.

His eyes are a light blue, like the color of the sky when it's filled with those beautiful white wispy clouds. He's moderately attractive, not cute like a little kid, but also not the hottest guy in the class. His brown hair is not buzz cut short, but not long and shaggy in his eyes. The most attractive part of Noah is his smile, it's like opening a portal into another world, where there are no outside problems. You can feel his kindhearted and humorous self bleeding into a room when he smiles.

The rest of the day is a blur as I'm so sucked in and mesmerized by him.

The faint jingle of the door, paired with a wall of joyous, bubbly laughter fills the small coffee shop, snapping me back to reality. It's hard to forget that it's Christmas time in this small town. The old brick buildings are decorated with dark green pine wreaths, each with a beautifully handcrafted bow tied around it. You can smell the fresh pine with every step you take outside. One of my favorite aspects of Fisher Creek is the peacefulness of being in the middle of nowhere. The lake is small enough that we have tourists all summer, just not an overwhelming amount. And even when the weather is unbearable, the humidity makes it difficult to walk outside without the sting of salty sweat dripping into your eyes. But no matter what time of year, the weather, or life, you can always head out to the lake for some much-needed rest and relaxation, especially when you've spent the last ten years living in the city and have avoided coming home.

Which is why I'm planning on hiding out in the coffee shop for the next few hours. Although I'm done with school and loving practice, I still take time to volunteer within the community by attending career days, volunteering at the school, and assisting the city community in any way possible. Caroline would tell you I don't have an off button and am struggling with the overwhelming desire to be needed by someone.

So I pull out my laptop and continue to work on the community luncheon I have in two weeks. I sit there, peppermint mocha next to my laptop, the opening slide of my PowerPoint staring back at me, unable to quiet my mind enough to start planning my next presentation.

Noah: "Drinks tonight?"

He's never been a man of few words but the last few years have been hard, distant even. It doesn't help that I didn't reply to his last message about getting together tonight. Pausing for a second, taking that big deep breath I practice with all of my patients when their exercises are difficult, I type back...

Me: "Sure, where ya thinking?"

Before I can even put my phone down, those dreaded three dots pop up, and I freeze waiting for his reply.

Noah: "I'll meet you at FishyBar at 7:30 pm?"

I can't tell if he's asking me or telling me. After the last time I saw him, I shouldn't be surprised by this. I shake that feeling quickly and respond.

Me: "That works, see you tonight!"

Then I quickly shove my phone into my bag so that I could get back to work.

FishyBar, I still do not understand who thought up that name for a successful business that has a reputation of being a busy spot, with a huge variety of drinks, poorly made drinks, that is. They trend on the side of strong, so strong you notice the taste of rubbing alcohol before anything else. The type of drink that you "who-wee" and crinkle your nose before you even take a sip. At least the wooden barn-style building was recently outfitted with a new heating system.

Fortunately, in the summer, Fishy's is significantly busier with tourist lake traffic coming from the bed and breakfast located at the far end of the lake property. They are known to the locals for their spectacular Christmas decorations that often illuminate the entire property, and with the new snowfall the reds and greens will reflect perfectly.

For a small town with very little population, we are fortunate to have a large area so everything is spread out aside from the town center. Heck, I'd argue there are more producing cranberry plants on our farm than there are people in Fisher Creek.

Our family cranberry farm is on the northeastern side of the town, the town center in the middle, and then the lake and FishyBar are on the opposite corner of Fisher Creek.

A few hours later I feel the faint grumble of my stomach and look down at the time on my computer, 1:30 p.m. The shop will be closing in thirty minutes and I'm sure my family is wondering where I've been hiding for most of the day. Plus, I should probably tell them I won't be home for dinner, and to certainly not wait up for me. I finish checking off my to-do list and pack everything back into my bag to head back home.

My car does not like the snowy, hole-filled dirt driveway as I drive toward the house. We have lived on this property for as long as I can remember. My parents, siblings, and I live in one house toward the front of the property, and my grandparents toward the back of the property. Our house is a white-paneled farm-style house, a dark green roof, with a beautiful wrap around deck. The dark wood panel deck reflects light perfectly into the main floor of the house through the giant windows surrounding the first floor. The property is mostly at the top of the hill and when you look down over the back there is an old, blue-green filled pond that my great-grandfather dug to fish with the kids over the years. Now this pond is covered with a few inches of ice and snow and hasn't been cleared off in ages.

I will always remember when the boys would employ me to help shovel the snow off as payment for being able to hang out with them and their friends in the winter. We would skate in circles around rough ice, getting endless scrapes from the roughness and contemplating ways to create an at home Zamboni for the next day.

Our ancestors' vision for the farm came to fruition over the years and I can only be so grateful that they planted a large family of coniferous trees lining the front and side yards of the house to protect the privacy of our family during tourist season. Now, as I pull back into the driveway those beautiful full green trees are dropping with the heaviness of the white snow, wearing it like a loose, droopy sweater to stay warm throughout the winter. They were set up as if they were two separate properties sharing the same driveway.

Since losing my grandmother earlier this year, the whole family worries about Gramps in that big house all alone. We have tried to convince him to move in with my parents now that I'm in Milwaukee and Pen is in Georgia. But the best we've been able to do is get him to eat dinner with us every night.

Losing Gram was easily the hardest loss to date, and I genuinely don't think I will ever fully recover from it. I wish the tears from my eyes. They come every time I think about Gram. I have no desire to have that conversation with my sister today. Penelope is the oldest of the four of us and since becoming a mom she mothers us more than anyone else.

Carter and Cole are twins, which runs in the family, here's to hoping it will skip our generation, the middle and then I'm the youngest of the four of us. Although there are four of us, I had the closest connection with Gram. We shared a love for baking and books and would even spend entire weekends nose down in our books together. As an adult that connection continued, even from two hours away. We had a standing phone call every Sunday morning to chat about the books we were reading, but in reality, it turned into Gram gossiping about the family and interrogating me about my love life. Thankfully, she never asked questions about Noah.

"Hey, Mom," I say as I walk through the front door into the kitchen placing everything on the table nearby. She's covered in flour as she attempts to bake holiday cookies. And yes, an attempt is an accurate description of what she's doing. Mom is a nurse by trade and has never been much of a baker. But we all love that she tries every year, especially now that the littles come up. We decorate them all together as a family, as a newer family tradition.

"Hi, baby," she replies, "How was your day?"

"It was good, I had a delicious peppermint mocha from the new coffee place and hunkered down to get some work done. When does Pen arrive?"

"She just called to say she's delayed...again...due to the weather and will be here tomorrow."

Pen met her husband in college and decided to move to Georgia to get away from the cold and the snow. In reality, I think she just needed a break from all of us.

"Oh, okay," I reply quietly, feeling disappointed. I love my sister but I only get to see her boys, a few times a year and am in dire need of some auntie time. "Noah texted me today..." I hear my voice tremble as I say this to my mom, and I'm thankful she is the only person around to hear me.

"Noah? I haven't heard that name in ages. Is he finally home from overseas?"

"Yeah, he got home last week. He wants to get drinks tonight at Fishy's. I'm going to meet him around seven-thirty, so don't count on me for dinner. And please, please, please, do not wait for me." I hear the creak of the old wooden front door open but barely have enough time to turn and duck before I'm pelted in the side of the shoulder with a snowball, courtesy of Cole.

"Come on, not in the house," Mom says as she chuckles.

Cole comes sprinting around the table to throw me into an excited hug when my phone buzzes and Noah's name pops up on the screen with a photo of us from high school. *I really need to change that photo from his contact information,* I think as I flip over the phone in hopes Cole didn't get the chance to see it. Too late, though. Cole's eyes grow big as a sheepish grin starts to slide across his face.

I know Cole really wants Noah and me to rekindle some resemblance of a friendship so he can have his friend back. Even though he would never actually pressure me to do so, being the protective big brother and all. Cole declared it would no longer be okay for him and Carter to be friends with Noah after everything that happened. Not that they even know the full extent of everything that happened. I still haven't told anyone the full story.

Cole reaches for my phone, knowing that I may have graduated summa cum laude in PT school but have the brain of a squirrel and will never change my passcode.

I swat his hand away and exclaim, "it's not what you're thinking. Do not give me that look," and then turn to walk run, rather, out of the room.

As I get upstairs to my childhood bedroom, I look around and see how my mother really has not changed a single thing, which is weird considering I'm now twenty-eight years old, and the teal walls definitely do not fit me anymore. Plus, I don't live here, so I'm surprised she hasn't changed the room into something more useful. I hurry to read my texts before one of the boys comes barging into my room demanding answers.

Noah: "Hey I know Fishy's is a bit from you, do you want to just park at my house and then ride together?"

Noah's text reads as if he is standing in front of me at school planning our weekend. I mean, he isn't wrong, Fishy's is pretty far from my house and he knows how much I hate driving down that way in the winter. The road is just a maze of twists and turns along the river. One wrong move, one small ice patch, and you're going to be swept away to the next city. But am I ready to be alone in a car with him?

Me: "yeah that works, thanks"

I reply before I have time to think too hard about it. I hear a knock on my door, assuming it's either Mom or Cole because I haven't seen Carter since getting in yesterday. He has grown distant and kind of mysterious over the last few years. I should probably talk to Cole about it since they at least both still live here and he would know best if something is going on that we need to address.

Cole is a volunteer firefighter for our town and responds to calls in the surrounding towns too. He also makes a point to come to visit once a month, which I can't tell if it's to check on my sanity or if he enjoys flirting with Caroline. But my money is on Caroline. Carter, on the other hand, has never really had any interest in anything outside of working on the cranberry farm. Which, in terms of Christmas makes him the easiest to shop for, because we just each get him new gear for wading through the cranberry crop. Now that I think more about it, I don't think he has ever been in a real relationship.

Our family has owned the cranberry farm for generations, my dad's great-great grandfather started it and it has stayed in the family since the start. Our parents were high school sweethearts, which is about as small a town as it can get. Mom is a nurse at the local hospital, which is actually like twenty miles away, so once we were all in school, she went back to work and Penelope kept us in line.

I hear another knock and since the door doesn't crack open with the second one, I know it's Cole. He's made that mistake once with Penelope and we will never let him live that down.

"Cole, get in here," I respond after the third knocking sequence starts. He opens the door, holding his hands together in front of him at his waist, which inevitably means he is apologizing for something.

He stands at the foot of my bed, where I'm leaning against the headboard. It honestly blows my mind how much Cole and I look like our mom, but Carter and Penelope look like our father. The small age gap between the boys and me means people often mistake Cole and me for twins. He remains standing there in silence in his jeans and gray crew neck hoodie. I know exactly where this going and I'm going to make him sweat it out a bit since we haven't talked since that night I was at the bar.

"Liv, I'm so sorry that I told Noah you were coming home," he says finally, looking up to look me in the eyes.

I want to respond with something witty and funny, but he looks genuinely sad, with big, green puppy dog eyes. Sometimes I wonder if Cole was a dog in a past life, and not one of those big mean dogs, but a big fluffy loveable one where you just want to squeeze their face. So I elect to be the kind sister that I am and not risk him feeling any worse.

"Cole, it's my choice to see him. That has nothing to do with you," I say, as reassuring as I can.

"After everything that happened in Oklahoma and you not really trying to date anyone else," he starts to say but then stops abruptly.

I narrow my eyes on him because I've made a point not to talk to him about my dating life which means he must be talking to either Caroline or Mason. I quickly weigh my options on whether that is a conversation or fight I want to have with him today and realize the answer is no. I make a mental note to text Caroline after this conversation and question how often she's in touch with Cole.

"I am just really sorry, Liv. I know he hurt you."

"Yeah, but it's not like we haven't talked in ten years. You know we text at Christmas every year," I reply.

"You haven't seen him in ten years, though, and I know you seeing him tonight stems from that night," he counters, looking at the edge of the bed, avoiding eye contact. So he was listening to my conversation with Mom.

"One: Stop listening to my conversations. Two: I'm an adult who can make decisions for herself. If I didn't want to go, I wouldn't. And three: I forgive you. So get that sad puppy dog look off your face and let's go help Mom with the cookies," I reply, wanting this conversation to be over.

I'm trying not to overthink about tonight. Though there's a pit in my stomach telling me that I really want to see Noah.

Chapter 6

NOAH

U sually running always clears my head and prepares me for anything coming my way, but after reading Ollie's text, I can't think of anything aside from the last time we saw each other. How terrible that ended, how our friendship stopped when I closed that door.

I don't regret that day, or my choice. I do, however, regret hurting her as deeply as I did and allowing our friendship to crumble under us. I follow her on social media and see everything that she's posted over the years, and I really couldn't be more proud of the person she has become. She is a doctor now while also making a difference in the lives of her community. She has a life in Milwaukee, sans me, with some friends who seem like they treat her better than I ever did.

"Are you going to tell her you're out?" my mom asks as she catches me looking at a photo of our family with Ollie and her brothers in it. We were quite the group of kids, always getting into trouble with the three of us and then Ollie finding some way to tag along. Sometimes it gets to me that Cole and Carter are not speaking to me anymore, and I barely get one-word answers from Ollie when we talk.

"I don't know. She lives in the city now anyway," I respond swiftly.

That's not the first conversation I want to have after being apart for so many years. The first goal needs to be to apologize and have a good time. To show her that we can be the friends that we were in high school.

Mom just shakes her head and walks away, and I immediately know she thinks that's the wrong choice. The one thing I've grown to love about my mom is her honesty. She will always let me know if she thinks I'm making the right choice, always supports the choice, and is always there to pick up the pieces when I have to admit that she's right.

Typically, around this time of year, we are getting new orders and preparing for our next move or deployment, so "retirement" feels foreign. Like there's a part of me that is missing. It has been three full weeks of being home with nothing to do and I'm starting to lose my mind. Living in the middle of nowhere has its perks when you're used to traveling the world but when you have to be here long term, I don't understand how our families have done it for the last hundred years.

I started volunteering with the volunteer fire company in Fisher Creek for something to do. The only problem is that Cole has been working full-time with the fire company since we graduated high school, and then helping out on the farm when he's not at the station.

Cole was one of my closest friends since I met Ollie, always hanging out with just the three of us, his parents even let me work on the farm the summer of our senior year so I could help my family out by making some money, and not have to worry about missing any soccer training.

But after that night in Oklahoma, the messages started to thin out and Cole and I became even more distant than Ollie and me. I can't blame him, Ollie is his little sister, and if he hurt Bec that badly, I don't even want to think about what would happen. I'm lucky he even said hello to me two weeks ago at Fishy's, let alone tell me that Ollie was coming home for the holidays. I'm even more grateful that he let me join the fire department, although I think it was mostly out of pity. It's still nice to be around him again.

Before I know it, I hear a shriek followed by laughter coming from the front of the house and I just know my sister has opened the door to Olivia for the first time in years. I know they still keep in touch periodically because she has a heart of gold, and whenever Bec and I are fighting, Ollie is usually the one Bec goes to.

I walk into the living room trying to make it seem like I'm calm, cool, and collected but can't help but stop and stare as I see her standing with her back up against the door, being bombarded by the pups. Her long chestnut brown hair falls with loose curls just over her shoulders. She's wearing a flowy, red turtleneck that sits right at the hem of her distressed black jeans. As she bends to give Archie his required head scratches, the back of her shirt slides up showing her olive skin. Milwaukee has changed her. She has grown up since I last saw her, she's filled out her body from that skinny preteen to a woman.

"Hey," I say, snapping out of a state of oblivion.

"Hey," she responds quietly, looking up from Archie, who proceeds to plant the biggest dog kiss on her cheek, causing her to burst into laughter. "I know, Archeroo, I missed you too." She's always had a silly nickname for the dogs, and I can't even remember how this one came about but hearing it again has my chest warming.

I chuckle and respond, "You ready to go?"

Ollie nods and politely says goodbye to my sister and the pups.

We walk outside, and I'm instantly self-conscious about the insane amount of ice on the old wooden deck and the state of my silver 2003

Toyota Corolla. I haven't lived at home full-time in over ten years, so it just sat until Bec was able to drive. Ollie opens the car door and slides into the passenger seat before I make it around to the driver's side.

I can tell she's nervous when I slide into the driver's seat of my old beat-up car because of the constant bounce of her leg, which shakes the entire car, and the impulsive need to endlessly twirl her hair around her finger.

There is relief in knowing she still has the same nervous tendencies as when we were in high school. I don't know why I suspected that this would be an easy reunion, that we would see each other for the first time in ten years and have it be with the same ease and comfort. I can feel my heart race, trying to beat out of my chest.

I've never had any problems starting a conversation with friends or strangers, and yet today I am sitting here in my car, speechless.

"Can you believe all this snow?" she says after a moment.

We have hit weather talk, basically the bottom of the bottom of small talk. And it makes me want to hit the steering wheel because I don't know how to fix this. How do you jump into the real world? The real conversations? The ones that actually matter and people care about or remember?

I remember back to something my therapist mentioned one day; *talk about something important, divulging something about yourself while leaving the conversation open ended and ready for a response.* Dr. Doyle has been life-saving in integrating back into civilian life these last few months. Talking to people after tragedy, loss, and while suffering from PTSD is nearly impossible, and I cannot imagine being here without his recommendations.

"After ten years in the desert, any amount of snow seems astro-nomical to me. Does it snow a lot in the city? I imagine that the river gives you snow similar to the lake here?" I respond, hopeful to pull out of this god-awful small talk we are making.

"Yeah, the river doesn't affect us nearly as much as the lake here," she responds before falling back into a silent stare out the window.

One of my favorite things about Ollie growing up was her deep love for the holidays. Between decorating, seeing lights, baking, and spending time with family she always lit up extra bright during this time of year, and it's obvious that this year is different.

I had driven to the farm a week ago for a meeting with Cole, and found that they hadn't put any of their holiday lights out yet.

"I am sorry to hear about Miss Sharon," I blurt out.

She turns and looks at me, seeming confused. Oh my god, why would I say that? I mean, it's true. I am sorry to hear about Sharon. She was one of the funniest ladies I had the pleasure to know. Small, smart, independent and opinionated, and the absolute best.

But the whole point of today is to rekindle our friendship, not bring up sadness and ruin the night before it even started.

"I am so sorry. I don't know why I said that. Not that it's not true. But...just...I'm sorry."

Her expression softens. "Thank you. And it's okay, talking about her is a good thing."

I nod, not knowing what to say but thankful the ride to Fishy's is short and the surprise for her is about to be revealed.

Bec mentioned that the loss of Sharon Bennett weighed heavily on the Bennett siblings, especially Olivia, who hadn't been back to Fisher Creek since the funeral. I know how much she loved Miss Sharon and the holidays and I want to bring some of that life back into her eyes and smile.

As we drive down the long tree-lined road leading to the snow-covered dirt lot, I know it's going to be perfect. The trees are each decorated with their own set of white Christmas lights that twinkle perfectly off the snow-covered branches and ground.

"Holy heck," Ollie exclaims as her big green eyes widen bigger at the lights.

I just smile, knowing there is more to come. Unlike Ollie, I have been back to the barn a few times over the past few years, catching up with friends, and hiding from some others, so the updates aren't new to me. Ollie never liked Fishy's at night, always complaining that was when all the annoying drunks came out to play, so I doubt she's seen all the updates Mark and Melinda have done to the place, including taking over the old bed and breakfast on the property.

As we pull into the parking lot, you can see the fire pit flame burning bright alongside the reindeer, pulling the sleigh display along the thick frozen lake. It's already dark but you can still see the twinkles of lights off the ice where the snow is cleared to play pond hockey.

"This is beautiful. They know how to put someone in the holiday spirit!" Ollie says quietly as she steps out of the car and turns to take in her surroundings.

I have never really noticed how her eyes get big and almost sparkle as bright as her smile. God, I would give anything to keep that smile on her face forever. But the wind blows, wiping that smile right off her face as a visible shiver slides down her spine. She's probably freezing, opting to wear a light jacket instead of a heavy Wisconsin windproof winter coat.

"Let's head in and get a drink," I say quickly, ushering her toward the door to get her out of the frigid Wisconsin air.

The parking lot is full, indicating it's probably busy inside, meaning we'll have to sit at the bar. I feel the frown forming on my face and quickly push it aside so Ollie doesn't see it. The music is loud; way louder than it was earlier this week. And that sound...

"Next up for karaoke: Kimberly M"

We hear as we open the door and step inside.

No. Not karaoke night.

Tonight cannot be karaoke night.

Chapter 7

OLIVIA

Karaoke.

Karaoke.

Did they just say karaoke?

Yep, they definitely said it.

My worst nightmare is now sitting in front of me. Singing in public. Absolutely not. I have always been a shy girl. I love music; give me the house to myself and I can guarantee you that I have music playing loud. Probably a little too loud. And I'm singing, also probably a little too loud. But I'm by no means a singer, I'm not good at it, and to stand up in front of a large number of strangers and sing is an absolute hard no for me.

But it's okay I don't have to sing, right? I can sit quietly at the bar with my drink and listen to everyone else sing. My internal monologue is going a mile a minute and I'm trying to avoid the panic from showing on my face. I was already nervous about tonight before karaoke was even considered.

"And for you?" the bartender asks, snapping me out of my head. He looks vaguely familiar and I definitely know him from somewhere, but can't place him.

"Oh um, just a gin and tonic please," I stammer.

"Just a gin and tonic? You don't want anything off the specialty menu?" Noah asks, surprised.

"I didn't know there was a specialty menu."

"You really don't come home much do you?" "Can you give us a specialty menu and a few minutes please?" Noah asks to the bartender.

"Not really, at least not in the last year"

"Ollie, Carter worked out a deal with Mark and Melinda, they source all their cranberries for their cocktails from you and make everything in house."

That is a huge deal for the farm, Mark and Melinda own not only Fishy's but the bed and breakfast that hosts basically every tourist we get on this side of the lake. The number of people our Cranberry Farm reaches with this deal alone is insane. It makes me proud to be a Bennett and of Carter, who has more formally taken over the farm, for getting a deal this big.

"You didn't know?"

I shake my head no. "Carter and I are more of the fight first and speak later type of siblings."

"I remember that. Ya'll used to fight like your lives depended on it and then Cole and I had to pick up the pieces."

The warm, homey feeling creeps back into my abdomen as mentions of our lives in the past, bringing me back to a time where he was my home. I love remembering back to those days, where the world didn't feel so heavy and it was just me and the boys conquering everything.

"Ready?" the bartender asks, coming back to us again.

"Yeah, can I have the Fishy's Fog? Please."

"And a float for you?" he asks Noah.

"Yessir" he says with a smile. I give him a pointed look in response.

"There *is* only *one* place to drink here" he says with a shrug.

He's not wrong. Fisher Creek is an incredibly small town, with basically one stoplight to get you through the center of town, but it is weird to imagine him here regularly.

"We have to sing tonight," Noah says to me as he comes from behind me to take the seat beside me.

"Absolutely not! I don't do karaoke," I respond.

"You used to love singing, you'd scream-sing as loud as possible in my car."

He isn't wrong. I'm comfortable with Noah, and we used to drive down this exact road to the lake with the windows down and the music fifteen octaves too high singing. I typically had my hair down and at least one arm out the window, dancing in the car seat as we drove.

"Yeah, in my house. I'll need about eight more of these to get up there," I say as the bartender passes us our drinks. "You go. You always sang just as loud as I did."

I should have known right then that this is going to be the biggest mistake of the night. The corner of his mouth rises into this competitive smirk as if he just won the lottery as he saunters off to the DJ stand. He signs himself up, and I swear he is laughing to himself as he walks back.

Noah is tall and strikingly handsome. The army really did a number on him, in the best way. Then again, what else is there to do in the desert? I've kept in touch with Bec over the last few years, even when Noah and I weren't speaking. She's my sister and it's not her fault that everything fell apart. I know he was overseas for the majority of the last ten years traveling all across the world with the U.S. Army. I know he was also stationed in Iraq for a few years but don't know much more than that. His clearance keeps him from talking about work a lot of the time.

But looking at him walking back to our spot at the bar, it's nearly impossible not to notice how big he is. He has always been super tall, but was considered lanky before boot camp. I guess, after boot camp is the last time I actually saw him in person, and he has bulked up a lot. Before, you could see the starting definitions of his muscles in his arms but nothing like it's now. He's wearing these dark blue jeans that fit his waist, backside, and thighs perfectly, and what's probably a white t-shirt underneath a dark hunter green sweater, with brown cowboy boots tucked away under his jeans.

His jawline is perfectly chiseled and his hair a dark brown wavy mess that's just long enough I could run my fingers through it, and that's exactly what I want to do. I always loved the idea of wrapping my fingers into the hair of my partner as we kiss up against the wall, but that's never an option with Noah because he always kept his hair short. This is certainly a pleasant surprise that I will be fantasizing over later after a few gins. Noah is fortunate to have perfect teeth and never once needed braces, which, to this day, I'm still jealous of. Even after two and a half awkward years of metal filling my mouth, my teeth are far from perfect.

"Don't worry, I only signed myself up...for now," he says, smirking at me as he finally reaches his barstool.

"You wouldn't dare" I gasp.

He just shrugs his shoulders in reply. There is something almost electric about being near him again. It's like we are two magnets with a constant pull near each other.

"Ollie, we should talk about..." he starts to say before I interrupt him.

"No, I don't want to talk about it. We haven't seen each other in ten years. Let's just have fun tonight."

His face drops as he looks down to me, and I already know he's unsure of how to respond. He's just going to apologize for Oklahoma, and the rain, and everything about that trip. I may still be hurt from that weekend but it's not going to stop me from having a great night, at the bar when I would otherwise be sitting at home staring at the ceiling. We continue chatting, people-watching, and listening to the people sing karaoke until we hear,

"All right, everyone, get ready for Fisher Creek's very own Noah!"

I cringe hearing this. The DJ knows Noah. He's done this before. I don't know why I'm surprised. Noah has never cared what anyone thinks about him and has always loved being the life of the party. Noah gets up to head over to the microphone, and I grab my cell phone to record and ask the bartender for another round.

The music starts, and Noah starts singing, and I'm instantly reminded that Noah, like his mom, can sing. And they're good. I feel the redness in my cheeks start to fade as a giant smile crosses my face. I find myself quietly singing along to the song hiding behind the camera, swaying to the music when I start to feel eyes on me. Not just one set of eyes, but many. I stop swaying, stop singing, and start to look around. The entire bar has now turned and is watching me, my face starts to heat rapidly and my eyes are getting big. The secondhand embarrassment from before begins raging through my veins again and the rumbles and tumbles in my stomach start turning.

Why are people looking at me?

"He's singing to her..." I hear the man three barstools down say to his wife. Her face becomes soft, and welcoming as if this is the cutest event she has ever seen. And then I hear it...

My eyes start to well up with tears. I fight back the emotions.

He is singing the Backstreet Boys.

This is not happening. Not here. Not now.

I don't hear the rest of the song. I don't hear anything until the song ends and the whole crowd erupts into clapping and hollering. The Backstreet Boys, I've always had a soft spot for their music but it's definitely more about the lyrics.

I fully expect to be transported into that moment years ago standing outside his hotel in the rain. The day we lost it all. I expect to be overwhelmed with emotions both good and bad. But it's an overwhelming warm feeling like I've come home.

I take my phone out to text Mason and Caroline before Noah makes it back to me.

> **Me: Guys…Noah just sang a karaoke song to me…at a bar in front of everyone.**

> **Mason: LOL! PLEASE FORGIVE HIM.**

> **Caroline: OMG!!! THAT IS ADORABLE. Get in his bed. Or I will.**

I quickly put my phone away as Noah approaches and I feel the fight of emotions in my brain take place. I struggle to decipher between being angry, after all these years, the first thing he does is sing me a song, and embarrassment, because I absolutely detest being the center of attention and now the entire bar is watching me and my reaction, and giddiness, because there is always some part of me that will be attracted to Noah, that will love him despite wanting to hate him, wanting to be angry about that day ten years ago but there is just something inside me that can't.

Clearly, the giddiness is winning with the sudden, almost uncontrollable urge to wrap my arms around his neck and hug him. Which is absolutely terrifying, but, honestly, fuck it. I'm only home for a few days and let's be real, he will probably be heading back to whatever country he is in now for the next ten years. What will one night of fun hurt? Nothing. I'll go back to my normal life tomorrow and this will all just be a memory.

Seeing as the giddy, happy, missing Noah side of my brain won, I jump off my barstool and directly into his arms, with our first true touch of the night.

He smells like cedar and sandalwood. My favorite scent, how did I not notice it earlier? I feel the surprise in his entire body as it tenses but it only lasts a split second before I also feel one of his hands on the small of my back and the other with a firm grip under my leg hoisting me into the air before he spins in a circle. I squeal and bury my face into his shoulder gripping tighter as a deep laugh escapes my body.

"God, I have missed that laugh," he says as he puts me down.

I try to remember the last time I laughed so deeply and genuinely. I know my life has changed drastically, I laugh with Mason and Caroline all the time. But this laugh is different, it comes from my toes and leaves me wanting more.

"I have missed you," I whisper, afraid to let him know, but curious if he missed me

too.

"Ollie...." he starts, and I start to panic as my shoulders drop toward my feet. "I have missed you every day since"

"Stop. Nope. I've missed you but we're not talking about that day. Not now. Not here," I cut him off before he can finish that sentence. That day is too painful and I've already vowed tonight to be fun.

"Ollie, we have to talk about it," he says quietly.

"Probably. But not now, not in public," I say, willing my voice not to break.

"Okay," he agrees, wrapping me back into his arms. "Okay."

We order more drinks, continue talking and listening to the people around us, and the music, and just take in our surroundings. The silence between us doesn't feel awkward or uncomfortable. He leaves his hand on the small of my back while we sit there. It feels natural and as if we're falling back into our old ways. After having a few "Fog's" as the locals call it, I'm feeling giddy and happy in his arms. I listen to Noah sing two more songs, the smile growing bigger with each song. Mark and Melinda, the owners, have popped out from the back a few times, trying to convince me to sing. Melinda even offers to sing a duet with me.

"Nope. Sorry, guys, not tonight," I say, taking a giant sip of my drink, coughing slightly because it's definitely more gin than juice. I know at this point there is no way either of us are going to be able to drive back to his house, let alone, me driving back to the farm tonight.

My heart rate skyrockets and panic starts to sink in. I know I can't drive home, but what am I going to do? Stay with Noah? At his house? No.

Chapter 8

NOAH

Holding Ollie is like holding the warm sunshine. One that I'm not ready to let go of. It's getting late but Ollie has finally relaxed into the night and we chat about her life in Milwaukee.

She may have lived there for the last ten years but still feels like a tourist so she, Caroline, and Savannah made a pact to do one thing a month to make them feel more like Milwaukee natives. Which is ironic because both girls are from big cities.

"Our townhouse is not far from the waterfront and one of my favorite things about the city is the way the sunsets over the water. It gives this perfect reflection of pinks and oranges into the river water that is just so calming and mind-cleansing after a hard day," she describes.

"That sounds so nice, we spent most of our time in the desert, so the last time I saw the sunset over water was...I don't even remember," I reply.

Her face drops, not with sadness but concern for me, and my life overseas.

"Being so close to the parks, bookstores, restaurants, and bars is one of the most convenient things and it is the one thing I'd miss the most if we move outside the city," Ollie replies with a hint of sadness to her voice. I stay quiet and continue to look at her as she elaborates "We have talked about moving outside of the city to a house with a yard for Gus, Mason's dog, but every time it comes up we end up right back at the convenience factor."

"Do you want to move out of the city?" I ask, genuinely curious.

"The short answer is no. Not immediately, having forever changing running trails, endless nights of live music, new restaurants, and monthly bookstore trips with Caroline are my entire life. They are the light in the hardest of days. Being able to come home, change, and walk to the park, place the blanket in the soft, vibrant green grass and listen to whatever local indie band is playing is like having a little piece of home it the city," she answers.

Ollie has always loved being outside, but small-town Wisconsin made it difficult to spend time outside in the winter, which was the majority of the year. Especially living close to the lake, we get a lot of lake-effect snow, and if it's not winter it's probably raining so being able to lose yourself in a fantasy world was her favorite way to hide away from the cold and the snow. Even as a child, when she was fighting with the boys, Penelope, or even her parents she often would "run away," later to be found on a small wooden swing hanging from a tree in the backyard just staring off into space at the pond.

"It sounds like you guys already know the real answer then," I say, unsure of why I feel disappointment with her excitement.

"Oh! And there is this really amazing margarita place, they have these skinny girl margs of various flavors. But the spicy cucumber jalapeno is to die for, literally."

She continues to talk about Mexican food, and girl's nights full of margaritas but I don't really hear anything else she says because I can't help but smile listening to her talk about her favorite city things, seeing how far she has grown since we first became friends in high school orientation. She has changed in so many ways. She's more outgoing, sharing her passions instead of sitting in silence, fighting the internal monologue of public speaking and ice breakers; and more beautiful than ever. God, she really is beautiful.

I always thought she was cute but she has changed and matured into this beautiful, independent woman. Her chestnut hair is long and flowy, but not too long to be annoying. Her olive skin is permanently tan, but smooth and soft to the touch. She's filled out perfectly from that rail-thin soccer player she was in high school. And she fits snugly into my side with my arm around her. Ollie's nose is slightly crooked from when she broke it during a state soccer game but refused to stop playing once the bleeding stopped. But what gets me are those big hazel eyes and her impeccable smile. They will light up an entire room upon walking in.

At a few points throughout the night I want to tell her about my orders or lack thereof but, I chicken out each time. I'm finally getting Ollie back in my life and I don't want that to change. I know it will, because after everything, she doesn't even want to talk about that night. She's still hurt and it's because of me, I feel my heart starting to ache knowing that I'm the reason for that pain.

My phone buzzes and I know that it's either Bec or my mom checking in regarding our ability to drive home, and I quickly shoot a text back that we're going to stay at the bed and breakfast here. Ollie's looking at me confused, like she received a similar text, when I realize they created a group chat. *Shit.*

"Ollie, neither of us can drive, the bed and breakfast is open and it's off-season," I say

"Are we sure that is a good idea?" she replies quietly.

"Yes, trust me," I say and when she doesn't reply I ask, "Do you trust me, Ollie?"

There is a brief pause in her response and my heart rate increases, worried that I've overstepped the invisible boundary we set tonight.

"Come on, let's get one more drink, I want to hear more about that park you love."

We continue to talk until we hear the barback yell from the doorway to get moving, and realize it's already almost 2 a.m and Fishy's is closing.

It took some coaxing but she finally agreed to stay at the bed and breakfast under one condition. She needs to be back at her house by nine to help her dad and brothers with something on the farm. Except it's already two in the morning and if we have to leave by eight, that means she is getting a maximum of six hours of sleep. I bet she is going to be a monster in the morning, without at least six or seven hours of sleep. She always was grouchy in the morning without sleep or a vat of coffee and I don't think she is going to get either. Whereas, I'm lucky if I get seven hours of sleep over three days.

We begin walking to the bed and breakfast through the frosted pathway. The walkway from the bar to the bed and breakfast was shoveled yesterday, but there is already a dusting of snow covering the walkway tonight.

The warm orange light coming from the steamed-over front window, paired with the smiling college student on winter break sitting behind the desk, and the welcoming atmosphere is why I've always loved coming to the bed and breakfast. The young man's smile grows when he realizes who we are, a perk of a small town, everyone knows everyone and will greet you with a smile no matter what.

"How can I help you?" he asks kindly, sounding a bit tired. We are likely the only people he's seen in the last five hours, and I'd be willing to bet he wasn't expecting anyone to walk in at this hour.

"We need a room with two beds for tonight, please," I reply, trying to emphasize the two beds part as quietly as possible. It has been eons since Ollie and I spent the night together, and there is a sudden sense of nervousness and anxiety that rushes over me that I did not expect twenty minutes ago when I suggested staying here.

"Okay, give me one minute to gather some information and we will get you checked in," he replies with a slight smile on his face.

After a few minutes of entering information, the young man hands us our keys to the room, and yes, they are literal keys. This house is a historical masterpiece in our timeless town, which means in order to make significant updates it takes a committee, a town vote, and about every step in between making the update not worth the investment.

Ollie unlocks the door swiftly and sneaks past. I push the door open and smack right into the back of Ollie as I walk in. She stops walking and is just staring into the dimly lit room. I place both hands on the outsides of her shoulders to ensure I don't knock her over and glance past her into the room.

One bed.

There is only one bed in the room, the room I specifically asked for two beds.

"I'll go back to the front..." I start to say realizing now why the kid at the front was smiling when he was checking us in. Ollie unfreezes and continues into the room.

"No," she whispers, with such sincere hesitation that you would think she is asking a question instead of making a statement.

I slowly follow her farther into the room and notice that it's also only a full-size bed, which is against the wall. Who the heck designs a room with one nightstand and the bed against the wall? Then I realize we are probably in the smallest room in this entire building.

"It's fine, we've slept in the same bed before. What's one night?" she asks.

"Ollie, I'll sleep on the floor," I say. After our hug earlier, I don't know if I can keep my hands to myself for the entirety of the night if we have to share the bed.

"Noah, it's a hardwood floor with a cheap old rug with who knows what on it. You're sleeping in the bed, you can stay on the outside and I'll take the wall." This is more of a demand than a debate, and I instantly know there is no winning this.

Looking around the room I notice there is a very old hunter-green velvet loveseat that would probably fit my torso and half of a leg, which is probably the "second bed" in the room. For a second I contemplate offering to sleep on it, but the second Ollie plops down onto it and grunts, I quickly nix that idea. She pats the spot next to her softly, indicating she wants me to sit next to her.

I can tell she is still feeling the alcohol by the haze in her eyes, the soft giggle she lets out as I sit next to her and the couch creaks as if it's going to collapse beneath us.

Ollie's quiet giggle fades into a deep, sad sigh. "I'm not ready for tonight to be over." She sighs as she leans her head against my chest.

I wrap my arms around the top of her shoulders and whisper, "Me neither."

Little does she know, I want to stay like this forever. Cause even after one night, after all these years, I'm still in love with Olivia Bennett and all I can do is hope she still feels the same.

We move to a more comfortable position on the couch where I'm against one side and she sits criss-cross-applesauce on the other side facing me, and we continue chatting. I tell her as much as I can about my time overseas, which is mostly just what life was like living in a desert on a cot for so long. Long story short, a lot of time in the "gym."

She shows me some houses she and her friends are looking at renting farther outside of the city. They want a bigger space so the dog has a small yard to run around, but all will miss the downtown lifestyle, which is why they haven't committed to one yet. As we continue to talk, Ollie inches closer and closer on the couch so that our shoulders are touching. She's curled up, sitting on top of her legs and feet and when she shows me a photo or a video or laughs, she leans in closer, resting her head against me.

"Oh my gosh, it's already four in the morning!" Ollie exclaims in a loud whisper, trying not to wake anyone in the house since the walls are thin. Good thing the only other person here is the kid at the front. "We have to go to bed!"

I feel my shoulders sink, knowing she is right but not ready to be away from her. There is a huge weight dropped directly onto me knowing this night is coming to an end but also a fear that I will never see her again. She'll get up early, and call Cole to come pick her up before I even know what happened. We haven't even talked about how long she is home for, or if she wants to get together again, or stay in touch or anything.

If I'm never going to see her again, I at least want the opportunity to say goodbye this time.

Chapter 9

OLIVIA

"**C**ome to bed," I say. There is no way I want tonight to end. I haven't felt this comfortable or laughed this genuinely in a long time. Plus it won't be the first time we've shared a bed, and secretly I pray it won't be the last.

"Ollie, I can sleep on the couch," he says, looking at me with what I think is a concern in his eyes.

"Nonsense, you sleep on that and your back will hurt for weeks," I reply as I grab his hand and start tiptoeing quietly toward the bed. I have to crawl across the bed to get to my side. He doesn't object this time and follows me to the bed.

The floor creaks, and Noah chuckles as I freeze, placing his hand on my lower back which sends a vibration through my entire body. His touch inches me farther onto the bed as he starts to take off his sweater. I slowly flip onto my back, watching as he gets undressed, and see he is also watching me with hunger in his eyes.

"Do you mind if I sleep in just my boxers?" he asks, throwing me the plain t-shirt he was wearing underneath his sweater. I barely catch the shirt because I'm mesmerized by his body, and am fighting the urge to place my hands on the defined muscles of his abdomen and chest. Quickly, I slide off my clothes and throw the big t-shirt over my head. Thankfully, while we have both grown, the ratio of size between the two of us has remained the same, and this shirt covers me perfectly.

I feel Noah's eyes watching me as I change, the hunger growing. Next, I throw my long hair into a tight bun on top of my head and wait for him to crawl into his side of the bed. This may be a full-size bed, but there's barely enough room for us both let alone room to leave any space between us.

It's December in Wisconsin, so it's cold, especially at four in the morning. But in the bed, next to Noah, there is endless warmth.

We are just sleeping next to each other. I have to convince myself but the warmth of his body next to me is incredibly inviting.

Screw it, I'm here to have a good night, and I probably won't see him for another ten years. I nestle close to him, tucking my head into the crook of his neck. I feel him tense at first but he quickly relaxes as I settle into my spot. His hands find the spot on my waist that makes me go weak. Even after all these years, he knows exactly where to put his hands, as if it's muscle memory.

We lie here in silence, as the tension builds between us. I finally tilt my head up to look at his face to see him looking above my head, seemingly contemplating. His face looks stern, but also welcoming and soft, like he's so deep in thought only a knife could penetrate it. I move one hand up between us so it sits flat on his chest because I want him to look down at me. He jumps as though I've startled him. He looks at me and is quiet for the next few moments.

Our mouths are no more than two inches away from each other. "Ollie," he whispers, "Can I kiss you?"

I smile, not even bothering to reply before I place my lips against his.

His lips are soft and welcoming, and he slowly plants kisses in a line from my mouth, down my neck, and along my collarbone. My body instantly responds, becoming wet and gripping fingers around his bicep, keeping him close. His initial question felt so innocent, only to be replaced by a ravenous, feral Noah I have never seen but want so much of.

He slides his hand up along my abdomen, kissing me so deeply, that I lose myself entirely as I slide a hand from his chest to the top of his boxers, lopping my fingers around the waistband wanting to see more of him.

"Off," I demand.

His hands remain on my body, tracing every curve, muscle, and crease through the shirt I'm wearing. I continue to trace circles down his abdomen and raise my leg draping it over him and rubbing my thigh along his already hard shaft, thankful he is as needy for me as I'm for him.

Placing his hands on my hips he flips us so my back is against the bed and he is positioned between my legs. My heart pounds with desire, and my pussy pulses in anticipation of what is coming next.

I need him. I need more. He doesn't move a muscle and the antic-ipation is slowly starting to kill me.

What is happening to me? Usually, I need Vlad to be even close to finishing, and right now I fear it might be over before we even start. The look on Noah's face is hungry and devious.

"I like watching you squirm," he whispers quietly into my ear as he traces a hand along the edge of my t-shirt slowly making his way up my thigh toward my apex. The sound that comes out of me is basically a whimper as he stops right before my entrance and it's all I can do not to buck my hips forward into him as he slides down placing kisses on my abdomen and thighs.

"Noah," I whisper between labored breaths. Christ, this man is going to be the death of me. At this rate he won't even have to touch me to finish me off.

I move my hand between my legs, reaching for my clit, needing something, anything but he quickly grabs my wrist and pins my hand at my side.

"No, that is solely for me tonight. Now, be a good girl and stay still while I worship this beautiful pussy of yours," he says with such a commanding manner that I freeze, and the bratty side of me wants to know what happens if I don't.

"And if I don't?"

"Bad girls don't get rewarded with orgasms," he says instantly, not missing a beat. "And then I have to punish you. And, Ollie, in case you don't remember, I'm impatient and need to taste you so be a good girl and let me eat."

Well, shit, that was hot. I don't think anyone has ever offered to reward me with an orgasm. And with the tension building inside me, I need this ache to subside, and I need it soon. I move my hips up again, trying to signal to him that I'm also impatient, when his tongue slowly flicks over my clit, and it's all I can do to stifle my moan.

"Fuck, Ollie, you taste so good," he says between circles of his tongue on my clit while the other hand gently squeezes my nipple. "I want you to come for me, baby. I want to have you all over my face."

Typically, dirty talk is a turn off for me, but when it comes from Noah Kneland there is nothing I want more. Now, pair it with the finger inside me and I'm overwhelmed with sensation and already too close to finishing.

"More," I demand, hoping he will finally take his cock and bring this all home.

He blatantly ignores me and continues working his tongue and fingers, curling them to hit the right spot, making it impossible for me to sit still.

"Relax, Olivia. Let it go. I can feel how close you are," he says, changing his tone from a demand to almost a plea.

Is Noah losing control too?

He pinches my nipple one last time and does that thing with his tongue, completely sending me over the edge. I lift my hips with one hand in his hair, and cling on for what feels like dear life as he feasts through my first orgasm and begins working for the second without even giving me a second to breathe or letting me take care of him.

Thankfully, he leans up onto his knees a moment later, sliding his boxers down. He gently slides his cock into my soaked pussy and begins thrusting back and forth.

"God, Ollie, you feel so good. This is never going to last, as long as you deserve," he pants, stopping right outside my entrance, obviously not using his full length.

"More. Noah, I need more," I plea, closing my eyes, and on the brink of my second orgasm.

"Open your eyes, I want to see your face when you come on my dick," he demands as he thrusts deep inside of me, this time giving me everything I want. Simultaneously, he swipes this thumb over my clit in a torturous circular motion sending me over the edge. I feel him fall over the cliff with me and I reach up and clamp my hand over his mouth to keep his roar as muffled as possible.

He lands next to me as we catch our breaths, and I feel like I have to say something. Having sex with Noah was not on my bingo card for this holiday season, let alone having the best sex of my life.

But what do you say to your ex who you just had mind blowing sex with after not seeing them for ten years? Thanks? Congratulations on being one of maybe five men in the world who actually know where the clit is? No. Nothing. There is literally nothing I can say aside from "that was amazing" and that seems too awkward itself.

So, instead I lie in silence for what feels like an eternity.

"Come on, Ollie, let's get cleaned up before we actually go to sleep," Noah says slowly climbing out of the bed. But at this point I'm too tired to move, so I grab ahold of his arms and beckon him to stay in bed.

"No, I'm too tired to shower now," I say, closing my eyes and nestling into the bed.

"You have to, otherwise you'll be complaining in the morning about how everything smells like sex. And do you really want to go help your dad and brothers smelling like me?" he asks in a snarky tone, knowing damn well that will get me out of bed faster than a bolt of lightning.

There is not a chance in hell I'm showing up at the farm and having to field that conversation with my father and older brothers, cause we all know Carter is never going to let it go.

After cleaning up I roll literally roll, back into the bed toward the wall and snuggle under the big comforter when Noah slides in next to me wrapping me in his arms for warmth. But secretly I think he also isn't quite ready to let this night end, yet.

♪♪♪

The eight a.m. alarm is entirely too early this morning, so I begrudgingly turn it off and roll over to slide off the bed. My head is pounding. I really shouldn't have had that final drink last night. I feel the hand resting on my hip as I roll over and instantly recall everything from the last four hours. The endless kisses, the laughs, and the amazing night of sleep.

Gosh, what the heck was I thinking, sleeping with him? Easily the best sex I've had in the last ten years but under no circumstances can it happen again. I only have four more days in Fisher Creek and I won't see him again after that.

Out of all the talking we did last night, I don't even know what his life looks like now. Did I even ask him where he is going next? I really don't think I did. I spent the entire time talking about my life, my favorite parts of Milwaukee, my friends, and everything important to me. I never even thought to ask about him or his life. What type of friend does that make me? Obviously not a good one. Is he going back overseas? Is he stateside now? Where is he stationed if he is stateside?

I shove my inner monologue aside because even if I want to continue this and see where things go, there is no way we can work, not after everything that has happened. I pause as the spins start to take over the room, and suddenly putting jeans on feels like an impossible task as my head rides the tilt-a-whorl around the room.

I look up and see Noah watching me, indicating I wasn't as stealthy in my escape as I thought and woke him up. The smirk on his face tells me he is finding my struggle amusing.

"Lose your balance, Ollie? I know the sex was good but I didn't think your legs would still be shaking," he says.

"The room is spinning, asshole," I bite back and finally get my jeans the rest of the way on.

"Serves you right for trying to leave without saying goodbye. How do you plan to get home? I drove us, remember?" he says as he jingles the keys on the nightstand.

"Fuck" I mutter under my breath. I really am off my game. How could I forget that he drove last night?

Chapter 10

NOAH

I find myself cursing the alarm, wanting to throw it through the window. Neither of us are ready to be awake yet and I had hoped we could just lie here for a while longer but my dream was interrupted by Ollie shimmying to the end of the bed trying to sneak out. I chuckled as she paused halfway through putting her pants back on, when she gave me a dirty look and complained about having the spins.

"Ollie, just get back in bed, you can help your dad in another hour," I say, almost pleading. Trying to emulate the voice she used to use when trying to convince Cole and me to let her join our activities. I'm hoping this isn't the formal goodbye.

"Noah, I can't," she replies quietly as her phone starts ringing. I look to see her dad's name light up the screen. Service is terrible here so she lets it go to voicemail but her pace quickens as she gets ready.

"Last night was great, and it was really nice to see you again..." she starts to say, gathering her purse and phone.

"No, this is not goodbye. How much longer are you here? I want to see you again," I reply with a hint of desperation in my voice. Hopefully, it's not too obvious how much I want her.

"I'm here for another three days," she says, slipping on her shoes. "Right now I have to get back to help Dad, I promised him I would. We can plan something later tonight," she finishes.

I begrudgingly crawl out of bed and put my jeans and sweater back on since I have to drive us back to the house so she can grab her vehicle.

Ollie shuffles us out of the room and down the hall before I even have my boot entirely on. I grab her forearm and stop her while putting them on and say, "Slow down, Ollie. Your family would rather you be late than in an accident."

She huffs a response of annoyance but slows enough that I don't feel like I'm running behind her. We round the corner into the lobby, she continues toward the front door as I hear "I hope you had a great stay, miss!" from the front desk. She doesn't even take a second to respond to him before walking out the front door.

"Sorry, we're running late," I mumble, handing the keys to the kid, who just stops and continues to look longingly at me as if waiting for a story.

"Is there anything else?" I ask, knowing Ollie is probably halfway back to Fishy's by now.

"Did you have a good night?" he says, winking at me, like he's my "bro" and we've been friends forever.

I can't help but laugh and shake my head as I turn and walk out of the hotel not giving this kid the satisfaction of knowing he absolutely set up the night and was successful all at the same time.

The wind is blowing swiftly brushing the dusting of snow through the air and into our faces. Ollie is standing at the top of the stairs of the deck with her hands in her pockets, shoulders up to her ears bracing for the cold trek back to the bar.

"Here." I hand her my jacket and put it over her shoulders and she shivers and looks up at me, with thanks.

"You're going to be cold."

"Probably but you'll keep us both warm," I reply, wrapping my arm around her shoulder, tucking her close to my side to step down the stairs.

By the time we get to the car, our teeth are chattering and our faces are red with wind-burn as we practically run to get the car started to warm up. There's also been a shift in the environment and energy of the day. Ollie pulls away from my arm leaving a cold chill, and she doesn't say anything as she gets back into the car.

I start the car and blast the heat to start warming everything up before I grab the snow brush to clean the snow and ice off the car. Looking at Ollie through the window, she has this distant, focused appearance as she stares out the passenger window. The pit in my stomach drops, wondering if she regrets last night, and then it falls even deeper with disappointment knowing that I don't regret last night and I would do anything to have it happen again.

"Ollie, are you okay?" I ask as I get into the car

"Huh?" she replies, obviously returning to reality from whatever planet her mind wandered off to.

"Where did your mind just wander off too?"

"Oh, uh, no where," she stumbles out, clearly embarrassed and unwilling to tell me what is going on in her head.

"Ollie, we have to talk about last night, and everything that happened."

"No, we don't. Last night was great but we're both going back to our own lives. There is nothing else to talk about," she retorts with a bite that I'm not prepared for.

"Ollie."

"I don't want to talk about it, Noah. I had a great time, let's just leave it at that."

I left it at that, even though the silence is screaming louder than any words would until we reach my driveway.

Ollie's in her car and backing out of the driveway before I even make it to the stairs. As I open the front door, the smell of coffee starts to warm my nose telling me that someone is in the kitchen. In my half-awake state, I imagine Ollie out there with a mug of coffee and a book sitting at the table, feet resting on the chair closest to her.

As I meander down the hallway, I'm greeted by Archie with his big, happy face and floppy ears. "I know, buddy, I miss her already too," I say as I scratch his head, knowing full well that he can smell Ollie on me.

"Did you tell her you're out? That you're signing the official paper-work today?" Mom asks as I round the corner. She and Bec are sitting at the small wooden coffee table in the breakfast nook off the kitchen looking at me like my parents used to when I tried to sneak in after curfew. Mom sips her coffee, glasses sliding down the bridge of her nose, looking over the top of them as the heat from the coffee steams them.

"No, Mom. We were just having a fun night, catching up," I reply, more stern than intended.

"'Cause that's why you're just getting home," Bec coughs out under her breath.

I can feel my face heat as the red starts to fill my cheeks.

"I tried to talk about Oklahoma and she shut down. She doesn't want to try, she just wants to have fun," I say.

"Sure. Well, the big Christmas party is tomorrow, invite her to it. I miss

having her around the house," Mom says as she walks out of the room to get ready for the day.

I know I have a meeting with my superior at 10:30 a.m. where I have an exit interview and then have to go to the local office to sign the official paperwork. By noon today, I will no longer be an active member of the Army, I will now just be Noah, a volunteer firefighter and veteran. I will be building my life in Fisher Creek, just a mere two hours from Ollie's city. The one where she created her home after I uprooted all of her plans.

I'll tell Ollie the truth tomorrow at the Christmas party if she comes. I grab my phone off the nightstand in my bedroom, realizing it's already 10:25 and I'm going to be late to this call if I don't get set up now. But first I send her a quick text.

Me: Christmas Party tomorrow, mom expects to see you there.

I lock my phone and pull out my laptop ready for this meeting.

"You're sure you're ready to be done?" Commander Gibson asks a moment later.

"Yes, sir. It's time," I reply with as little hesitation as possible because, in reality, the Army is all I have known for the last ten years. All my friends, brothers, and everyone outside of my immediate family are in the Army.

"Very well. We will miss you, kid," he replies. Commander Gibson is the closest thing to the father I've had since joining the Army, and leaving him feels like losing a piece of me. "You always know how to reach me if you ever need anything," he adds quickly. We're both trying to hold back all tendrils of emotion. "You need to go into the office today to sign the paperwork, officially retiring you from the United States Army," he finishes.

"I have a scheduled appointment with them at eleven-thirty to finish everything today," I reply. "Thank you, sir, for everything." Well, it's officially happening.

I check my phone, seeing her name and photo on the lock screen. She replied about the Christmas party. My stomach starts to twist as I dread her saying she doesn't want to come, that this is over. I never would have taken myself as an anxious person, but something about Olivia turns my entire brain and body to mush.

> **Ollie: We have our family Christmas Eve Dinner tomorrow night, but can I come early to help set everything up?**

My chest warms and the tumbleweeds in my stomach relax knowing she wants to see me again. This time will be different, and I will not lose her again.

> **Me: Great, be here at 1 p.m.**

Chapter 11

OLIVIA

The entire drive home all I can think about is last night and how it was everything I didn't know I needed. I know one thing for certain. I'm not ready to let go. Deep down, I know I want more. I shake my head free from the fantasy and realize I need to separate myself from Noah for the remainder of this trip because in three days we'll go back to holiday and birthday texts only.

A giant wave of sadness flows through me when I consider the real possibility of that. One night with Noah has me entirely unraveled, ready to jump back into his arms, and never let go. But I know that is never going to happen. He's only home for holiday leave before shipping back to wherever he is deployed at this time.

I learned very early after his first deployment that I can't imagine him over there, in the desert, with the hot, dusty air filling his lungs and the endless danger. The endless danger that takes the lives of so many people every day. It was maddening, heartbreaking, and all-consuming for the first few months. Not knowing where he was, if he was okay, and listening to the news regarding what was happening overseas. So, eventually, I decided it was safer not to. Safer to not think about it, disconnect and not look up the details of the war. Even though I created that necessary distance allowing me to grow, focus, and be successful within my career; there has always been part of me that worries, part of me wonders if he will get out or if he will let the Army all consume his life, like I let it consume mine for so long.

"Olibia!" I hear a tiny voice shout as I get out of my car and start walking toward the house. Liam, Penelope's youngest, comes running out the front door straight for my knees. Part of me hopes that he never stops calling me "Olibia". Growing up, my family either called me Olivia or Liv except Penelope, who always called me Olivia. She is a firm believer in using a full name. Our family are the only ones who were able to shorten Penelope to Pen and that's only because Penelope is a long and difficult name for a toddler to say and there were three of us running around, needing her. Her children are Liam and Leo, never anything shorter, and her husband's name is Jonathan, not Jon or Jonny.

"Liam, let Aunt Olivia get into the house before you attack," I hear Penelope say from the doorway. A half smile rises on her face, knowing that I'm both surprised and excited to see her.

I share the same quick smile. Having not seen her since the services, which we did not end on great terms, there is a wave of sadness that overwhelms the smile. I have always been "full of feelings" so the coming and going of the ocean is nothing new for me.

"I thought you weren't going to make it until tonight or tomorrow," I exclaim, trying to remember back to what Mom said yesterday, while also wondering why I drank so much gin last night.

I haven't seen my sister since she left after Grandma's services and we had gotten into a fight about her going back to Georgia already.

She wasn't as close as I was with our grandmother and I used that to my advantage in the argument. We didn't speak for almost two weeks before I caved and called her repeatedly until she answered. I may be the annoying little sister but family is everything to me and I couldn't survive without her. She's my confidant, my informant, and one of my best friends. Seeing her this morning is exactly what I need.

"We were able to find an earlier flight!" she responds, and I jump into her arms to give her a giant hug.

"I'm so glad you are here!" I say burying my face into her shoulder.

"I'd never miss an opportunity to be the first to hear about how you spent the night at Noah's," she says, smirking.

My family has always been Noah's biggest fan, and I know the fight put a damper on all of them, especially Cole. Knowing that he is somewhere upstairs waiting for my return to hear if he can be friends with Noah again, makes me grateful that Pen intercepted me at the door. I'm definitely not ready to tell my brother about last night, especially the fact that we slept together.

"Pen...it was..." I start, not sure where to begin or how to describe how I'm feeling. "Everything," I finish, dropping my arms from her, shoulders starting to slouch. There is a bone chilling gust of wind causing me to shiver, making me wish I had elected for a warmer jacket when I realize I'm still wearing Noah's jacket from this morning.

My face blanches as Pen smiles and says, "Come on, let's get inside."

Pen is the only person who knows everything that happened on that dreaded night in Oklahoma. She knows how broken I was and was ready to fly back to Milwaukee to pick up the pieces, after making a pit stop in Oklahoma to see Noah. It took a three-hour FaceTime call, with Pen, Jonathan, Mason, and Caroline, a bottle of wine, and lots of laughter to convince her to stay in Georgia.

Liam pulls his train set out and is driving it along the downstairs bonus room floor, so Penelope grabs my arm and pulls me over to the couches. The dark gray fabric couches have been in this room for as long as I can remember. And while they are about as worn as the cheetah print attitude shirt with a monkey on it that I wore in middle school, I would be devastated if my parents ever decided to replace them. Our entire childhoods are in these couches from the fights to the tears to the holidays.

Once we sit, Penelope says, "Tell me everything, Olivia."

And so I do.

Chapter 12

OLIVIA

"That bastard," Cole exclaims as he runs down the stairs to me crying while explaining the night before. "I'm going to kill him," he adds.

"Easy there, killer, he didn't do anything wrong and did not hurt her," Pen says, putting her hand up and motioning for him to come over and sit on the other side of me. After finishing the story, explaining how I feel and everything else, we arrive at one conclusion. I have to tell Noah two things and follow the one rule we set in place for the remainder of this trip.

1. Tell Noah how I feel

2. Tell Noah we cannot continue

3. Do not have sex with Noah (again)

"These rules seem easy enough," I say, letting out a ragged sigh, wiping the tear stains on my flush freshly cried cheeks away.

My siblings look at each other and scoff a slight laugh before turning to me and saying, "Sure" and "Easier said than done, Liv."

"What do you mean?" I ask, confused.

"Olivia, honey, you and Noah are like two magnets that are constantly drawn to each other no matter how far apart you are placed. It was like that when you were kids, I can't say it is going to be any different now. You can't deny the magnetic field, Liv. You're a doctor, you know that's not how science works," Penelope replies.

"It wasn't always like that, he hated me when I first met him," I retort, but before I can even finish the part about us defying it for the last ten years, Cole bursts out into the deepest laugh I have heard from him in a long while.

"You think he hated you?" Cole gets out between laughs, and Penelope swats him on the arm.

"Yeah? He was the one to always say no, when I tried to hangout with you," I say, confused.

"Oh, Liv, Noah only said no because you're my sister and he thought it was weird to be attracted to his best friend's sister. He just tried to keep the distance to help himself," Cole says, and my mouth basically drops to the floor.

"Wait, what?" I ask glaringly.

"Yes, Olivia. Who was the first one there for you when you fell and scraped your knee? Or when Matthew was a dickhead to you? Or when you and Penelope had a big fight? I can assure you, it wasn't Carter or me, although we were a close second," Cole shares again.

I am so confused… Why would he not tell me that? I always thought he hated me until I was in high school. Did Cole give him the okay? I think back to that day during my final cranberry harvest, how did that day even happen?

I guess there were signs that I just didn't see. Maybe I ignored them.

"Did everyone realize this but me?" I ask quietly, feeling a mix of guilt and sadness that I didn't put the two together before then.

Penelope and Cole just shake their heads in disbelief.

"Everyone, Liv, literally everyone. That's why no one was surprised when you started "dating" in high school," Cole says.

My face heats with embarrassment and I hide my face in my hands willing this feeling to go away. I feel overwhelmed and silly for not realizing these facts in the moment and feel myself sitting here reliving every moment between Noah and I from the last twenty plus years of my life.

Sure, with every fall, every fight, literally everything, he was there. I know he was always at our house between his friendship with Cole, parents being busy, and then working at the farm, I just thought it was just a coincidence not that he was actually being present.

I can't help but stop at one memory that is glued to the back of my eyes. Penelope and I were fighting in her bedroom, I was sitting on her bed, demanding to get ready with her as she was getting ready to hangout with friends.

"Olivia, get out of my room," Pen yells without turning her face from the round, perfectly lit mirror hanging on her vanity. She pulls a tube of mascara from her pink and yellow makeup bag and begins applying it.

"No, I want to do makeup too," I reply, crossing my arms and sinking deeper into her bed.

"You're too young for make up," she snaps back, acting like Mom, who is working late at the hospital tonight.

"Mom would let me wear it," I say, hopeful that she'll let me join in.

"Mom isn't here and this is my room and my makeup and I'm telling you no. Now, get out." I can tell that her patience is thinning but I just want to be included. Being the youngest is the worst because the boys have each other and their friends, who want nothing to do with me and Penelope is six years older than me, so our lives are so different.

"Please, Pen," I cry

"Now, Olivia."

"Why?"

"You're my lame ten-year-old little sister, I don't want you hanging out with me or my friends. We are too different and you're too young. Get out now before I have to drag you."

It wasn't a particularly brutal fight between us, we've certainly had worse, but what sticks in my memory the most is the aftermath of it. Penelope did end up pulling me out of her room and then locked the door behind her so I couldn't get back in. But the worst part was in the upstairs hallway was Cole, Carter, and Noah standing outside their room, looking in my direction. My face reddened with embarrassment as I couldn't keep the tears from filling my eyes and blurring before I took off down the stairs and ran outside.

I had made it to the swing in the back part of the yard overlooking the pond when a gentle hand was placed on the rope of the swing, turning it slightly.

"Hey Liv," the familiar voice said but I was too embarrassed to look up.

There was silence for a moment before I finally looked up and saw Noah.

Noah Kneland, was standing in front of me with a sorrowful look on his face.

"What do you want?" I said through tears.

"Just wanted to see if you were okay?" he asked tilting his head to one side, looking into my eyes.

"No. No one ever wants to hangout with me. Pen hates me. The boys have each other and you and then there is just me, alone. Why do you all hate me?" I blurted out through labored breaths.

"Liv, no one hates you," he said pulling me off the swing into a hug. I wrapped my arms around his waist and continued crying into his shoulder.

"She okay?" Cole asks from behind us.

"She's slobbering all over my shirt, Cole, what do you think?" Noah responded. His comment pulled me out of my stupor and made me chuckle.

"Sorry, Noah." I responded when I pulled my head away and dropped my arms.

"Come on, kid, why don't you come hangout with us? We were about to take the cart out around the farm." He said, and wrapped one arm around my shoulder and turned us toward Cole. Cole instantly wrapped his arm around my other shoulder and we headed to the barn.

The rest of that day was one of my favorite memories of us all as kids. We rode the carts around the property for hours, singing, the wind blowing through our hair. Cole driving through the mud puddles and tried to spray us all with the spray before we had to clean the car which turned into a water fight.

Through everything, Noah was the first one there.

The first one to react.

The first one to care.

The first.

Chapter 13

NOAH

Olivia walks in the front door and it's clear to me something is different. When I hug her, it feels quick and distant like she's pushing away and shutting me out of her life. Her smile and demeanor are quiet, and polite, as if my tongue wasn't in that soft spot between her legs two days ago. Something is definitely wrong, maybe she regrets that night.

She's wearing a pair of black yoga pants and an oversized red and white Christmas sweater, her hair is pulled up in a claw clip with pieces falling around her face. She is wearing large clear square glasses, making me smile because Ollie always hated wearing her glasses when we were in high school.

"They make my face look pudgy," she would whine, whenever we asked her where they were or if she could even see anything.

But these glasses fit her face perfectly and make her look professional, but cozy.

She turns to look at me as she slides off her fuzzy slippers and I instantly clutch my chest, shooting her a shocked look.

"Glasses? Has the world ended?" I gasp at her.

"Ow, you wound me," I say after her slipper hits me in the shoulder.

She smirks and pushes past me toward the kitchen where Mom and Bec are arguing over where the green olives should be on the cutting board.

"Ollie's here!" I shout to the kitchen, hoping their banter will stop as I close the door. I follow her, finding it impossible not to stare at her beautiful body. I barely make it in the kitchen before I notice the green olives are now being placed in a clear glass jar next to the cheese wheel and the pastrami slices. Ollie has this magical ability to diffuse any situation around her, and has always been a problem solver to a fault, sometimes.

Bec quietly retreats to her bedroom. While she loves helping and setting up for these big events, she needs time to herself before they happen. They tend to be full of people, asking so many questions about our lives and what our plans are and it's always the people who do not actually give a shit but are just nosey and just here for the drama. That also means tonight will be the night the whole town learns I'm home for good this time, so I have to tell Ollie before she leaves today. I'd rather she find out from me than someone else.

I sit up on the counter and watch Ollie and Mom decorate the charcuterie board. They're laughing and making jokes about who's going to show up in the most ridiculous Christmas sweater this year. My money is on Gary from down the road.

It's nice to see them together again in the kitchen, it reminds me of the old traditions we had when they'd cook together before a party and then yell at me for picking food off the platter too early. But hey, a growing boy has got to eat.

"Gary. One hundred percent, Gary. He's like the weird, friendly uncle that nobody wishes they had," I say.

Ollie swats my leg and Mom gives me a scolding look before Ollie says,

"Leave Gary alone, he is widowed and has no one. Christmas is his favorite holiday," Ollie exclaims. She's always looking to see the good in people.

"As long as his sweater doesn't sing again," Mom says, laughing.

It's at this moment where I really can see a future here in Fisher Creek with Olivia. It's the first time that I can see us together planning out our lives and spending time with both our families. I long for the continuation of that relationship, reconnecting with Cole and Carter and constantly fighting off Penelope's sisterly threats.

Ollie brushes up against my leg as she passes by to put the cutting board in the sink, and sends an electrifying shock through my body, pulling me out of my fantasy.

As she walks back toward the counter, she brushes against me again, this time with a devilish smirk on her face. She knows exactly what she's doing. So I slide one hand around her waist and pull her close, nestling her into my body. I feel the instant tension but hold her tight and place a gentle kiss on the top of her head. Two can play this game, and I don't like to lose.

Her face turns bright red, even as she relaxes into my hold. I know it's because Mom's in the room with her back to us but still Ollie is embarrassed. She's never been a fan of PDA although before this trip our touches had been mostly innocent. I can see the corner of my mom's mouth turning up, happy to see our playful sides coming back. She's always wanted Ollie to be part of our family, *officially*, even before I did.

Mom quietly excuses herself to get ready for the Christmas party, leaving Olivia and me alone in the kitchen. Using my hand on her waist, I spin her around so she's facing me. Her face is still bright red, but she looks up and places her hands firmly on my thighs, pushing up toward my face, and plants a kiss on the side of my face.

I jump off the counter, backing Ollie up against the wall behind her. I place one hand on the front of her hip, and the other around the back of her neck. She lets out a gasp as I lean in to kiss her. But before I get to her mouth, she has both hands gripping the front of my shirt pulling me closer. I kiss from her lips down the side of her neck as she lets out small quiet moans telling me I'm hitting the right spots. Ollie starts moving her hips against the front of my jeans.

"Damn, Ollie," I rasp. She stops for a moment, grinning. Before she can start again, I wrap my arms around her waist, throw her over my shoulder, and carry her into my bedroom. Using my foot to close the door, I throw Ollie onto the bed but she has a grip on my shirt, pulling me on top of her. I kiss her deeply with my hand wrapped on the inside of her thigh. She moves her hands toward my belt and starts to unbuckle it.

"This time, it's my turn to worship you," she says with a smirk.

♪♪♪

We're lying in bed, Ollie's head resting on my shoulder, with one hand sitting on my chest, when she sighs deeply, full of emotion.

"Noah, we can't do this again," she finally says, filling the silence.

"What do you mean, this?" I reply, not sure if she means the earth-shattering sex or hanging out.

"All of it, Noah. I live in Milwaukee, no one ever knows where you are going to be. There cannot be a this or an us, and you know it, too," she says.

"Ollie…" I start to say as her eyes start to get watery. She has always been a crier. When she's sad, when she's happy, when she's angry. Tears. But my chest starts to tighten seeing her crack open like this. "I'm staying stateside, this can work. I want this. I want you." I finish.

"You got out?" she asks quietly.

"You're looking at a newly retired US Army Veteran," I reply.

"When?" she demands.

I don't answer right away, coming up with the best way to tell her this has been in the works for weeks, but only official as of yesterday.

"When did you get out, Noah?" she asks, again.

The sentence is gentle, but the tone and urgency in her voice tells me I've made a mistake. At this point, she is sitting up, facing me, hand no longer on my chest.

"Officially?" I say quickly. "Yesterday, but I have known I was retiring since I came home two weeks ago. I'm staying in Fisher Creek. We can finally do this."

Silence.

She doesn't say a word as she jumps out of bed and starts getting dressed.

Not one word.

I don't think I breathe a single breath either.

Chapter 14

OLIVIA

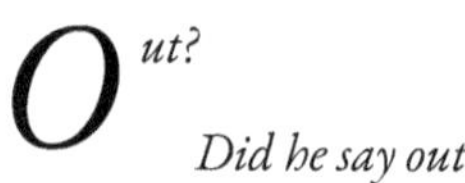*ut?*

Did he say out?

No.

Absolutely not.

Why wouldn't he tell me that the other day?

Everything is a blur. I can see him talking but can't hear a word he is saying as I get dressed. The buzzing in my head gets stronger and louder the longer I'm in this room. My chest has a vice grip on me, and I feel like I can't breathe. I need to get out of here.

I set rules. And I broke the biggest one.

"Ollie."

"Ollie."

"Olivia," he gently yells. He's out of bed and standing in front of me, his hands are reaching for my shoulders to stabilize me.

"I need to leave." I stammer as I start to push past him.

"Olivia, you're freaking out. You aren't leaving yet, let's talk this out. Get some fresh air and let's talk about it," he says.

I know he's right, but I can't think. I don't want to talk about it. He is staying in Fisher Creek, only two hours from Milwaukee. My city. My home. I don't have to see him, but I want to. I know that we'll be drawn together in that city or even back here, and I will fall again and he will leave, again.

I wasn't enough ten years ago, so what has changed now?

He'll just leave again.

"You want to talk about it? Noah, you left me. You didn't want me. I told you I was in love with you. *You left me.* No, Noah, the answer is no," I shout.

His arms drop from my shoulders, and I know I hit home hard. I high-tail it out of the house, pulling the door of my rental car open as quickly as possible before the tears start running down my face.

I'm instantly back to standing outside, crying in the rain in Oklahoma ten years ago, trying to find a hotel that wasn't fully booked with Army families.

Unable to tell if the salty taste I have in my mouth is due to the current stream of tears or the sting of the memory from all those years ago. *"Olivia, you should leave, we are never going to be together,"* I hear him say, standing outside the enormous glass windows of the beautiful hotel we had booked to celebrate.

My heart aches as I gasp for air through the heaviness of my tears. There is no way I can drive home like this. Not yet.

I close my eyes and rest my head on the top of the steering wheel trying to get myself together before heading home for the day, when I hear the passenger door open and feel someone slide into the front seat. I don't have to look up to know it's Noah, who is now sitting next to me in silence. Giving me space, but also showing me he's supporting me. The car door closes quietly but he still doesn't say anything.

We sit in silence for a few moments before I finally pick up my head, and glance at Noah. The skin under his eyes is puffy and red. I jolt upright and turn to face him.

"I'm sorry, Noah. I shouldn't have said that," I say quietly.

"No, Ollie. You're right and I have regretted it every day since then," he says, his eyes getting watery again.

I hate seeing him like this, I don't think I've ever seen him this emotional. I don't even remember him crying when his father died. I don't know what I can say to him.

Does he regret it? It's been ten years. Maybe he has changed, maybe things are different. We absolutely cannot make any decisions currently when I can still smell the sex on both of us.

"I cannot talk about this right now, Noah. I need time to process everything. We will talk before I leave," I say, gently placing my hand on his forearm, and watching his glossy eyes move from staring out the windshield to my face.

He doesn't answer right away, obviously contemplating whether or not to let me leave right now. I have to know why he retired, the Army is his entire life.

"Why?" I continue.

He sits in silence as if he doesn't want to answer that question, what could have possibly happened that would warrant retiring?

"It was time, Ollie," he says quietly, barely a whisper. There is something about the way he says it, a sense of urgency, hurt, and heartbreak. It's clear he doesn't want to talk about whatever happened, and after the added hurt I caused today, I don't want to push him.

If we're going to do this, he will have to trust me with the information, to be his support system, but it's also important not to push him.

A lot of things could have happened to cause retirement and it's not fair of me to demand answers when I can't give them myself.

"I head back to the city in two days so we will talk before then. But I need time, Noah, and I have to get back for my family's event," I say. My hand is still on his forearm and he's placed his opposite hand on top of mine. The touch is so innocent, genuine, and calming that I begin to crave more of it.

Noah releases my hand, and I, his forearm. He stumbles out of my car trying to stay upright and not slip on the ice below. He makes it to the deck before he turns around to watch me pull away. I wave innocently, and instantly am sad to be leaving.

Chapter 15

OLIVIA

"He's staying home," I say to Caroline while we talk on my drive home.

"Ol, so what? This is the perfect opportunity to explore what could have been," she says. She takes her job as my best friend extremely seriously and is always ready to talk me off my hypothetical cliffs. She is also usually the one with the rational brain cell.

"What if he" I start before she cuts me off.

"No. Nope. No. There is no what if," she says, "You've spent two days with him and it's all you have talked about. Obviously, there is something there," she finishes.

"Car, he left me standing outside, in the rain, in Oklahoma alone. How do I even come back from that?" I ask, genuinely curious about what she says. Caroline may be the rational one but she rarely gives second chances.

"Ten years ago!" she yells, leaving me grateful the Bluetooth in my car allows me to control the volume. "Olivia, people change. Have you even talked to him about that night?" she asks. I can tell she's getting annoyed but also know it's reasonable because she's probably right.

"No," I say quietly. Remembering back to the other night, the first embrace he wrapped me in saying we have to talk about it.

"What? What was that?" she asks knowing she absolutely won this discussion and that I would have to have this conversation with him.

"He wanted to talk the first night together but I wasn't ready. I'm still not ready," I say, almost ashamed.

"Olivia, you cannot keep living in the past. I know it's going to be an uncomfortable conversation and it's probably going to suck. And knowing you, you're going to cry, but you cannot grow without being uncomfortable. So go get uncomfortable," she says.

I know she's right but it took me months to pull myself out of the hole after Oklahoma, with the help of Caroline and Mason. Am I interested in opening that door up again?

Yes. My brain instantly screams yes. There's no hesitation in that answer. I sense the smile emerging on Caroline's face through the phone, yet again but we both knew there's only one answer moving forward.

"Thanks, Car," is all I need to say before hanging up the phone. I park the car in the driveway of my parents' house and immediately grab my phone to text Noah.

Me: Friends, let's start there.

I may not be ready to start a relationship with him yet, but the least I can do is work toward rebuilding the friendship we once held, where we were able to be in the same place without feeling an awkward tension pulling us together. Even if I think that tension is always going to be there.

I slide my phone into my pocket and look out the windshield. Pen and the boys are sledding down the hill behind our parents' house, Cole and Carter are standing at the bottom, watching me in my car. I see Cole lean over and say something to Carter, and everyone starts smiling.

And for the first time since being back in the dreaded Fisher Creek, Wisconsin, I'm happy. Genuinely and wholeheartedly happy to be here and for what is to come.

Chapter 16

NOAH

I need to run. I need to do something. But as soon as I walk back into the house Bec and Mom are in the kitchen again. They're getting ready to hang the decorations for tonight, most of which they can do without me, aside from the string lights Mom hangs on the old wooden beams of our house for "ambiance" or whatever.

They both turn to look at me, faces dropping as they see me alone, assuming what happened. I'm in no shape to have a family gossip session and hang lights right now, so I turn down the hallway, walk back into my bedroom, and try to close the door gently. But instead, it slams, the whole house shaking.

Our house is old but has been renovated over the last ten years, with the exception of the outdated wooden beams and the hardwood floor that Mom is obsessed with. The interior walls are an ivory color and the brick fireplace is now gray stone with warm terracotta tones to accent the wooden beams. Everything ties back to those damn wooden beams.

Lying on my bed and looking up at the ceiling I realize this is the only room in the house Mom didn't change much. She took the typical teenage boy stuff off the walls and repainted them but it's the same navy-grey color it's been forever.

I sit up and move to the large lounge chair I used as a teenager to read and play video games in. The bed smells of coconut and lavender, like Ollie's conditioner. I swear she hasn't changed the scent since high school. She always smells like a tropical beach.

The sound of quiet footsteps fill the hallway and stop outside my bedroom door. There's a 50 percent chance it's Bec going back to her bedroom, or someone coming to summon me to decorate. I'm not in the Christmas spirit, and I don't want to see people tonight. I'm looking forward to finding Archie and hiding in the corner of the room, watching everyone in my hometown gossip and judge each other.

There's a small knock on my door, and I just know it's Bec coming to find out what happened and too see if I'm okay.

"Come in," I shout as my phone buzzes.

The door creaks open and Bec peers in, looking apprehensive about coming into the room, as if things were flying around. Okay, maybe it happened one time. I don't have the opportunity to look up to further acknowledge she's here before I read the text.

Ollie: Friends, let's start there.

I can feel my facial expression changing but I'm not sure what exactly I'm feeling. I've never been great at sharing my feelings or emotions until therapy, after another comrade passed away. Then I learned I have lots of feelings, and learned how to classify them and triggers for specific ones.

This is different, this is a mixture of relief, happiness, and anxiety all in one. What are we giving a go? Past me would say she's giving me a chance to be friends again. But maybe she wants to just talk about Oklahoma.

"Breathe, control your face," Bec says, coming into the room and closing the door realizing that something has happened. I throw the decorative pillow at Bec's face and just stare at my phone.

"She's giving me a chance to be back in her life, Bec," I whisper, not entirely sure this is happening.

"How is that a bad thing? You looked like you lost your dog when you walked back inside," Bec says.

"I told her I was retired, and she panicked and ran. I thought I lost her forever, Bec. I know I just got her back into my life…but it feels real, like everything's clicked into place and the look on her face made me anxious in a way I haven't felt in a long time," I answer.

Bec may be six years younger than me, and we haven't always been so close, but I'm incredibly grateful to have her, and the relationship we have built.

Bec is my best friend. She has always been the support system, holding our family together, especially after Dad passed.

Bec comes over and gives me a very light hug. We're not a hugging family so it's odd she's hugging me, but also feels very right at the same time.

"Come on, ya big sap, Mom needs you to put the lights up," she says lightly, pulling me out of my chair.

"Those damn lights are going to kill us all one day," I reply.

Before we get too far out of the room, I text Ollie back.

Me: You won't regret it, Bennett.

I'm not letting Ollie go, she let me back into her life and I will do everything I can to stay there forever, even if I die in the friend zone.

I put my phone in my pocket and head to the living room to start creating the right ambiance for the party. I know Mom loves hosting this party year after year, and being able to maintain Dad's favorite holiday tradition, but sometimes I wonder if it's time for us to create new traditions.

Chapter 17

NOAH

"What is Ms. Fleming doing?" I ask Archie as I lean against the wooden beam in the dining room, looking through the archway to the living room. Archie's sitting at my side and he takes one paw to scratch the side of his nose.

"I know, Archie, I can barely stand to watch it either," I say, chuckling to myself. Ms. Fleming lives on our street and is in her fifties with gray-silver shoulder-length hair. She's never been married but is the town flirt. Watching her sit on the arm of the couch, leaning around Gary, trying to flirt with him is painful. So painful I can no longer watch.

Although I'd rather Ms. Fleming and Gary be occupied with each other than come over to my side of the house and interrogate me again.

"Oh shit, Archie, I spoke too soon, here they come," I mumble looking down at my best friend of a pup, who is about to run away before Ms. Fleming squeezes his cheeks and flaps his ears back and forth.

"Noah! It's so good to see you home," Ms. Fleming calls as she walks through the archway into the dining room.

"You too, Ms. Fleming. Gary, I hope all is well," I reply as politely as possible.

"A little birdy told us you're sticking around this time around?" Ms. Fleming asks with a sense of attitude I'm not ready for.

This is a topic of contention with the people who live on this dead-end wooded street, worsening after Dad died.

"True, signed the papers yesterday," I answer, hopeful that not feeding into her nonsense will at least put it to rest for the night and avoid causing a scene.

"It's about time you stay home to take care of your family. Maybe you can convince the Bennett girls to move back since you already got behind one of them," she says with more aggression in her tone this time.

It's one thing to be angry with me for leaving, but to bring Ollie and Penelope into this conversation is a whole other thing. And not one I tolerate well at all.

"Doris, leave the boy alone; it's not his fault the girls left town." Gary steps in quickly. "Noah, we're so happy to have you home, are grateful for your service, and lucky to have you on the local fire squad," he finishes.

"Noah, there you are, I've been looking for you everywhere. I need your help with some ice." Mom swoops in out of nowhere, and I don't know if I've ever been more grateful to be freed from a conversation.

I'm a mix of emotions, primarily confused and angry. I haven't told anyone about the fire squad, aside from Cole and a few of the other guys on the squad who would have the same shift as me and that's only because they see me every shift. The pleasure of living in a small town is that your business is no longer your business, it's everyone else's business. And that's going to take some time to get used to again.

"Thanks, Mom," I say as we head from the dining room into the hallway by the front door, genuinely grateful she saved me from that dreadful conversation.

I wouldn't say I have anger problems, but insulting my family is a really fast way to tick me off.

Ms. Fleming is not only the town flirt, but the town gossip who might as well be a reporter because she'll use any means necessary to get the story. Any story that can be shared with her book club to get her some extra brownie points.

"We all know Ms. Fleming, but after that comment about the Bennetts', she's lucky I didn't throw her into the snowbank outside," Mom replies with the hint of a smile at the end.

I can't help but laugh, imagining my mother, the small, former pole vaulter, politician's wife, throwing the frumpy Ms. Fleming over her shoulder and into the four-foot-tall snow mountain in the driveway.

"Well, I appreciate it," I reply. "I'm guessing you mean the ice in the driveway, so all these idiots can leave."

She nods. "They need to leave at some point."

"The sand mixture is right below the deck. I'll get right to it, if you start rounding up the troops to leave," I say.

Looking at the clock as Mom walks away before I head outside, I see it's well past seven and I start to think it's weird I haven't heard back from Ollie after my last text. But I also don't want to bother her, since she's with her family. I miss being able to just pop over there when this shit show of a party gets to be too much to handle.

Ollie's family always spends Christmas Eve with her grandparents at their house, having dinner, doing gifts, and playing games. This is the first year without Miss. Sharon and it's going to be weird for everyone. I can only imagine the state Ollie is in. They were the best of friends, and I hate that I couldn't be there for her during that time.

We used to split our Christmas Eves, starting at our familial events and then either I would go spend time with her and Cole, or she and Cole would come here. We would play board games, watch Christmas movies deep into the night, eat holiday cookies, and drink spiked hot chocolate, hiding it from our parents' every time they came to check on us.

Now that Penelope has two kids herself, I imagine someone is dressing up as Santa, and setting out snacks for the reindeer, which was always a favorite activity. I can just imagine everyone sitting downstairs near the giant, chaotic, but full of life and love Christmas tree, laughing as the boys open cars, trains, and fake power tools. Then Carter would take one of them outside to pretend to cut branches off the snow-covered trees.

Our Christmas' looked vastly different as children, Ollie's was full of life and family, whereas mine was full of egocentric community members pretending to be family. My father was a very well-known community member, and even ran for mayor once, so all of our big holidays were centered around the community and bringing the community together. I remember the parties being lively as a child. I would dress in green corduroy pants, with a white button-up and a Christmas sweater over it so that the collar of the shirt was sticking through. Bec would always fight Mom on her black, red, and green plaid dress she wore because she hated to wear dresses. But back then, everything was for show.

Once Dad passed, the parties changed. Mom does everything she could to continue the legacy of Dad's festivities but also gives us more leeway in expressing ourselves. Tonight I'm wearing very dark wash jeans with a red holiday sweater on top, whereas Bec's wearing leggings and knee-high riding boots, dressed up with a long green sweater that's shorter in the front.

We both know Mom isn't ready to let these parties go, even if we no longer want to participate in them, because it means letting go of a piece of the love of her life. But these parties are getting old, attendee numbers are down, and usually, there's at least one person at the event who becomes the story of the night, and never a good story at that.

It's a conversation Bec and I need to have with Mom since Bec's graduating and moving out soon enough. And with me moving into my new house, there won't be anyone here to support her.

I realize I haven't seen Bec in at least twenty minutes and while our house is big, these parties are not that big where she could go missing. I begin to meander through the remaining people and down the hall toward our bedrooms. I can hear the television in Bec's room and know she somehow managed to escape into her bedroom. This means I'm going to retreat into mine to hide for the remainder of the night. I'm all peopled out for the evening.

My phone buzzes as I waltz into my room and plop on the bed, Archie sneaking in right behind me.

> **Ollie: so so sorry it's been so long! I was playing with the boys and put my phone down and lost it and all the things. But I'm really excited for our friendship.**

Chapter 18

OLIVIA

It's well after 9 p.m. when we finally get the boys settled from a night of chocolate, games, and presents. Even telling them Santa won't be able to come if they're awake didn't work. We always do family presents on Christmas Eve and Santa presents on Christmas Day. It's nice to have little ones in the family again to do Santa on Christmas day again.

I spend the entire afternoon chasing Leo and Liam around, wiping chocolate off their faces, building train tracks, and running trains through their courses. We went outside to go sledding but I got too cold too quickly so we had to come inside. Spending time with the little ones is the best part about being home this holiday season. Living in Milwaukee is amazing, but also very taxing on family time when your littles live on the opposite end of the country.

I've always known Penelope wanted a large house and a large family but never imagined her living so far from home. She practically raised the boys and me, both of our parents working busy full-time jobs.

Maybe she just needed a break from the cold and the winter, from the craziness of always being responsible. But seeing her interact with her two beautiful babies has been nothing short of amazing.

The patience that I never remember her having with me is extraordinary, especially when the boys are at each other's throats and constantly calling for "Mommy." Do children ever call for their father? Her big blue eyes, and auburn-colored hair that's pulled up in a tight bun with loose strands framing her face, are always calm, with the most welcoming and loving expression.

I can't help but smile watching them interact and play on the floor. Halfway through the afternoon, I can tell that Pen is tired the boys are refusing to ap and she needs a break. She deserves a break. It's odd that Jonathan isn't here to help out or celebrate with us but when I asked Pen about it, she just brushed it off as work.

"Why don't you two come lie on the couch with me and we'll read a book?" I ask the boys as they come running out of their room for the fifteenth time avoiding nap time.

"You don't have to do that," I hear Penelope say as she rounds the corner.

I try my hardest to give her my best "you need this" look as Liam and Leo come running over with books. Pen knows how much I love books, so if I get to spend time with my littles doing my favorite activity, then it's the best day.

The laughter that comes out of the boys as they jump onto the couch and wiggle into comfy positions waiting for me to take my spot in the middle is the light of the holidays. It's so full of happiness and joy, and I'm curious if our laughter as children had the same effect on the adults as these boys do on me. I smile at Penelope and plop into the couch right between the boys. You can tell they're both overtired by the way they giggle at everything, especially the fact that spicy salsa is a hard no for our favorite dragons in *Dragons Love Tacos*. We make it through the giggles of dragons, but only about halfway through *No, David!* before there are two sleeping boys and an aunt who's definitely trying not to doze off with them.

"Y'all are too quiet..." Penelope says as she rounds the corner and I quickly bring my hand to my mouth to shush her before she wakes the beasts. She smiles, grateful the boys are napping but also how cute we all look curled up on the couch together.

I roll my eyes at her and say "Help me up so we can have spiked hot chocolate."

"Honey, you're not getting up until those boys do." She chuckles as she walks out of the family room. Knowing she's right, I lean my head against the back of the couch and try to relax. I'm going to have to go see my chiropractor when I get back to Milwaukee after this.

I feel my phone vibrate against my leg and gently try to wiggle it out without waking Leo who is now lying with his head flat on my lap. Once I get it out, without even looking at it, I place it face down on the side table next to the couch, and close my eyes pretending to be asleep as Liam begins to stir against my side. I know if he sees Leo and I sleeping, he'll just close his eyes again.

Turns out I'm sleepy too.

Chapter 19

OLIVIA

One minute I'm in a deep slumber, the next I'm being jumped on by a tiny three-year-old monster, yelling at the top of his lungs for me to wake up. How long was I asleep? It looks dark outside, but it's also winter in Wisconsin, where it gets dark at 3 p.m. Looking over at the clock I notice it's just barely after 6 p.m.

"What's going on, buddy?" I ask, half awake, trying to regather my surroundings.

"It's time to eat!" Liam yells in my face. I've never seen a child so excited for dinner before but then I remember the rule: dinner first, and once everyone's finished eating, we're allowed to open presents. I was really happy to hear that we're following typical traditions with the little ones, even though Gram isn't here anymore.

"Okay, let's go wash up then," I say, grabbing his hand and leading him to the bathroom down the hall.

When we make it to the dining room, I have to hide a gasp at how truly stunning the table setting is. There are beautiful poinsettias one on each side of the table. There's a new white with dark red embroidery tablecloth, and the table is set with beautiful white places and gold placemats for each person. Mom has made a honey-glazed ham, the most delicious looking garden salad with homemade Caesar dressing, garlic mashed potatoes, macaroni and cheese for the boys, and green beans. My normal spot next to Cole is open and waiting for me, with Pen waiting on the other side. The faint Christmas music in the background is the perfect touch not too loud to take away from family conversations at the table but just loud enough to be heard.

"This looks amazing, Mom," I say as I sit down. She only smiles faintly back at me. I've always loved being a part of a big loud family and am extremely fortunate to be part of a family that is loving and accepting of all my weird quirks no matter what.

The back door opens and a giant gust of air comes in, chilling the room. As the door closes behind Carter, we can tell he must've been out with some friends based on the smell of cigars and beer. His seat is on the other side of Cole, next to Grandpa so he has to squeeze past me to get there, and as he does, he places two frigid hands on my shoulders giving them a big squeeze and shake.

"Hey, look who decided to actually join us for a meal," he says. Carter has always been the brother who gives me the most shit, which also means we are the two who fight often.

"Caught up with some friends I haven't seen in a while before heading back to the city," I reply as nonchalantly as possible.

If Carter knew I was with Noah it would go one of two ways. He'll either be extremely supportive or he'll tell everyone he's going to beat up Noah for hitting on his sister again. They never got into actual fights as kids, but I know it was a common statement made between them. Noah would usually reply with some childish banter about having to be able to catch him, or that he would like to see him try. But after everything, I wouldn't be surprised if he was serious.

"Friends, huh?" he replies with one corner of his mouth starting to lift. Cole elbows him in the side, and I just continue to scoop myself a bowl of salad. "I heard today that you've been with Noah all this time," he continues.

You can hear a freaking pin drop, it's so quiet. Everyone's stopped what they're doing and are just staring between the two of us to see what comes next. Mom's face paled with disbelief.

I guess this is probably the first real interaction Carter and I have had since I've been home. While Carter and I love each other we were the fighters of the family, especially with each other. We would play a game as children to see who could push the other's buttons the most, clearly Carter never got the memo the game was over.

I could let him embarrass me, or I could just tell him the truth. Tell them all the truth. I still have feelings for Noah. I haven't even said those words out loud to myself yet, so I would prefer if they weren't dragged out of me by my annoying brother.

Nope. Not ready for that explanation and who even knows if it's going to work?

"Wow, Carter, I'm so glad you understand friendship finally," I retaliate back quickly. "Noah's retiring from the Army and is home for good," I finish.

Carter's smirk fades off his face, meaning I've won this round but not without further interrogation from Mom.

"He's staying home?" Mom asks with hesitation in her voice. Thankfully, silence can only last so long with two small children clanking their silverware on their plates.

"Correct," I reply, looking down at my plate.

"And how do you feel about it?" Mom asks hesitantly. She's always been one to advocate for us to talk about our feelings, thoughts, and everything going on in our lives. Which is great, except when you haven't decided how you feel yet and don't want to tell them the entirety of the story. She knows the majority of the story and how I handled it so I'm not surprised by her concern but I also just want this conversation to be over.

"Fine, we've been friends forever, it will be nice to be able to catch up now and again," I say as I spread butter on a piece of homemade bread. "Let's eat some food so these boys can open family presents before Santa comes."

Everyone begins eating, and I feel a hand on my leg. Penelope's attempting to comfort me. She can tell I'm anxious as my leg continues to bounce. She'd normally yell at me to sit still, but instead she whispers into my ear, "Tell me all about it later," realizing something has changed since we set the rules.

I spent so much time with the boys today that I forgot to text Noah back. I start patting my pockets, quietly looking for my phone, and can't find it anywhere.

I'll have to find it after dinner, to text Noah back, preferably before Carter gets to him or we become more of the town gossip.

Chapter 20

OLIVIA

I wake up to the sound of little feet pitter-pattering down the hallway and stairs onto the main floor of the house. The smell of freshly made cinnamon buns fills the air, along with the smell of bacon. It's Christmas morning in the Bennett household and that means a big family breakfast full of everyone's favorites. I swear my mother doesn't even sleep ever during the holidays. How she has the time to get all of this done and still look immaculate is beyond me.

I roll over, grab my phone, and begin my mindless morning scrolling through social media when Noah's text banner comes across the top screen of my phone.

> **Noah: Merry Christmas, Ollie! Let's plan something before you head back to Milwaukee!**

I can't help but smile at my phone with excitement to begin this adventure. But also just spending time with Noah takes me out of my rain cloud. Although, my rain cloud has quickly turned stormy when the car service reminder pops up on my phone.

I leave tomorrow morning to return to Milwaukee and need to get the car serviced before going back to work the following day. There is no way I'll have time to see him before I leave. My shoulders begin to sag as I respond.

> **Me: Hi, good morning, Merry Christmas! I leave in the morning.**

I'm sure to add a few crying emojis to show I'm bummed about having to leave. Never in my life would I have expected to be sad about leaving Fisher Creek behind.

But never have I ever left Noah behind in Fisher Creek.

Chapter 21

NOAH

Christmas has never been my favorite holiday, especially since Dad died. Our typical breakfast traditions fell by the wayside and the entire ordeal felt more operational than celebratory with family time. The ceremonious Christmas Eve tradition is the only tradition we've continued and it's as if that's too overwhelming to do anything else.

Mom always sleeps in after being exhausted from hosting and cleaning up from the party. She never lets us help clean, classifying it as her antisocial decompression time. Plus "we have to go to sleep if we want Santa to come," Yes, she still uses that excuse even though we're adults.

Mom firmly believes that the magic of Christmas never dies no matter how old we are. I lost the magic after the second Christmas when Mom couldn't get out of bed to celebrate with us. Bec may not remember that day, but that was when my family truly started calling me the Grinch.

I can't help but roll my eyes and chuckle to myself, knowing how true it is but also how different this morning feels. This morning, there's a new sense of excitement, and joy getting out of bed today. I can only assume it's due to having Ollie back in my life. I throw on a pair of gray sweatpants and saunter into the kitchen to get some caffeine.

"Who are you and what have you done with the Grinch?" Mom asks, turning with a cup of steaming jo to hand to me.

I laugh, take the coffee, and move to sit at the bar table while we wait for Bec to get up. It tends to be a slow morning, and if I remember correctly, I heard Bec sneak out around 1:30 a.m, which means we won't see her until the afternoon.

"Honestly, I'm excited to start this adventure with Ollie. It has been a long time coming... and I just hope we can get past Oklahoma," I say, realizing that this is real life and I'm about to reclaim a friendship I never should have allowed to fail in the first place.

As reality sinks in, my excitement and joy doesn't fade. They transition into an anxious excitement, remembering back to a few days ago when I envisioned the future with Olivia. I want to be the best for her but also for her found family. I want them to all see that I'm here for Ollie and I'm not going anywhere anytime soon.

I may not know Caroline, Savannah, or Mason but I know Penelope and Cole, and if they're anything like the first two, it won't be an easy transition back into Olivia's life. It's worth the fight.

I need to see Olivia before she heads back to Milwaukee, we need to talk about Oklahoma and clear the air. She needs to know that I loved her then and never stopped.

Sipping my coffee in the breakfast nook, with Mom reading the newspaper in silence is my favorite way to spend the morning when

I'm home. It's quiet and peaceful and Mom is too preoccupied to care that I have my phone out at the table.

> **Me: Merry Christmas Ollie! Let's plan something before you head back to the city!**

I've only been home for two weeks and I have learned two really important things:

1. I'm still in love with Olivia

2. I cannot under any circumstances live in my childhood house with my mom and little sister any longer.

Staying at home was always convenient for leaves, but they never lasted longer than a week. Don't get me wrong, I love my family and would do anything for them. But I need space and quiet. I need something to do with my everyday life when I'm not on shift at the firehouse or out on a call.

I want a place to call my own so I have been looking for a fixer-upper in the area, and trust me there are plenty. In the last two weeks I've looked at six small single-family houses but only one felt like it has the potential to be perfect.

It sits on the back side of town closer to the farmlands, on one and a half acres, with an old wooden rail fence surrounding the property. The house itself is one story, with a two-car garage, three bedrooms and two bathrooms. The master bedroom sits in the back of the house with a large picture window overlooking the backyard. The biggest complaint is that it's very closed off. There are at least two walls I'd like to knock down. It needs some TLC throughout the inside and then there's the fact that I haven't told my family I'm moving yet.

Well, frankly, I haven't told anyone I bought it yet. It's been empty for years, so I purchased it as is. I can get my keys as early as tomorrow.

I look up at Mom reading the paper on the other side of the table in the kitchen and feel guilty for not telling her yet. I know she'll be happy for me, concerned that I'm making a crazy choice based on everything that has happened in the last six months, but supportive nonetheless. She's going to want to help with anything she can, painting, decorating, etc.

"I bought a house," I blurt out. A wave of relief washes over me as I see her glance up over the top of her glasses, peering over the newspaper. Her graying hair still hangs in messy curls around her face. The expression she wears reminds me of my grandmother.

"Really? Where?" she replies with a hint of shock in her voice.

"On Tailer Road," I reply quietly. "It's the old Kinney property, it needs some love, but I need something to do," I continue.

"Are you sure you're ready to live alone? It's only been six months since Jarred...and only three weeks since you stopped having nightmares," she says, sounding genuinely concerned.

Fortunately for her, I have already talked to Dr. Doyle about this and we've concluded that it's both a positive outlet for any anger and confusion I have regarding Jarred and a way to grow into myself and immerse myself into the community. Plus, I have fulfilled the one thing Jarred asked me to do: meet with Ollie. Well, that isn't exactly what he asked me to do, but close enough.

"Yes, Mom, I'm ready. Dr. Doyle agrees and I promise I'll still come home and let you know if anything happens," I try to reassure her.

"Well, good. I'm proud of you, Noah," she says with a slight smile, proving she genuinely believes me.

My phone buzzes on the table with a text from Ollie:

Ollie: Hi Good Morning Merry Christmas! I leave in the morning.

Which is followed by a plethora of crying face emojis. I feel the disappointment wash over me, but I know she's only a few hours away and we'll plan a time soon to see each other, whether I come out to the city or she comes home for a weekend. However, the idea of not knowing when, where, or how that will all happen is terrifying.

I finally have her back in my life and it feels like she's running away again. At least I know I have something to keep my mind busy now besides sitting at home with Bec.

"I can get the keys in the morning. I'm going to start the renovations tomorrow, kicking it off with a fresh coat of paint," I tell Mom, trying to hide the disappointment in my face and voice.

"Well then, we better get you packed and ready. I'll get some food ready to send over with you in the morning." I've always had an amazing mom, she may not have been the most present after Dad died, but there has never any doubt in her love for her children.

"Thanks, Mom, I'm going to get some clothes packed. I doubt it'll be livable tomorrow, but some progress is progress," I say as I walk into my old bedroom.

Chapter 22

NOAH

While packing a bag of clothes and the desk objects for the new house I find a small tin box tucked into the top drawer of my desk. I remember unpacking this when I first got home two weeks ago and stashing it somewhere out of sight out of mind. Opening the small tin, I unfold the letter, dropping the dog tags from the inside onto the white oak desk.

Kneland,

If you're reading this, then you know what it means. That doesn't mean you get to blame yourself for this, for me. There is nothing you could have done to change the outcome.

This is typically when I stop reading, throw the letter back into the box, and tuck it far away. It has been six months since the ambush, the gunfire, and Jarred's death. It took me four of those months to even read past this part, which I have only done one other time, aside from today.

Jarred was my best friend and brother, he was family. He never had a family of his own, so he devoted all of his time and energy to the Army. Lived, breathed, and died for the US Army. We were the closest thing he had to a home, a support system, and everything in between. He was able to travel home on leave with me a few times and being a southern boy visiting the middle of nowhere Wisconsin was quite comical. He had never seen snow until he came home one year right after Christmas. That was also the first time he learned about the history of Olivia and me, only two months after Oklahoma and two weeks before we left for our first deployment.

I will never forget the look on Carter's face when Jarred and I walked into Fishy's that night, already feeling the Jameson we had at home, laughing and being a little rambunctious. I have known Cole and Carter forever, and while Carter and I were friends, it was nothing like the friendship I shared with Cole. Carter always took Ollie's side and would protect his family until the day he died.

We're walking into the bar. I'm laughing with Jarred about some pointless joke, and turn to see Carter sitting at the bar. He turns to see who's walking into the bar, obviously waiting for someone but when he realizes who it is, his entire demeanor changes. He's always been the tallest and slimmest of the siblings, but tonight he looks mean, like one of those men waiting at a biker bar for someone to walk in so they can rock their world.

"Kneland, why does that guy look like he's going to murder you?" Jarred asks cautiously, but also with a hint of intrigue.

I didn't know this at the time but Jarred was a fighter, he was the person at the bar we always had to back, which was ironic considering he probably the biggest, most built and gruff looking out of us all. Which always ended in people believing he was all talk and no action. He always stood tall, chest proud, and when he let his facial hair grow, he looked even more intimidating. Thankfully, he wasn't feeling particularly feisty that night.

"That's Ollie's brother," I say, I haven't spoken to Olivia or her brother since that night, and I knew there was not a part of me ready to face Carter.

Carter sets his beer bottle on the bar and pushes his stool back, getting up from the bar and walking toward us and the high-top table I snagged at the far side of the building. He stalks menacingly to our table and stops directly in front of me. He stands at six-five, so he makes my six-feet look and feel small. He stands there silently for what feels like an eternity, before jamming a finger into my chest, uttering, "You fucked up" before bumping into my shoulder and stalking out the side door of the bar.

"Man, what the hell was that?" Jarred demands. "I know something happened with Olivia when she didn't come back to the hotel after graduation, but what was it?"

"Nothing," I reply, not wanting to have to relive that night any more than I already am.

"If I'm going to have to defend your ass at a bar against that man, I need to know why" Jarred replies with a slight chuckle. This was a huge turning point for our friendship. Yeah, we went through basic training together, and we ended up going on the same deployment and squad, but sharing our personal lives never came up. They hadn't been important, I knew he didn't have anyone to call family and that was it. But having someone willing to back you up against a total stranger, when you deserved what's coming to you, that's another type of friendship.

"We need more Jameson for that story," I say.

Jarred goes up to the bar and orders four Jameson shots for us and once he gets back to the table, I tell him everything.

Putting down the last shot glass, I felt a sense of relief, sharing with someone what happened and the truth behind why it happened.

"You're an idiot. Noble as hell. But an idiot," Jarred says after a brief pause.

I have no words for his statement. He didn't say anything I didn't already know.

"I get why you did it, but, damn, dude," he says, looking down at the table, with one hand on the shot glass when I don't respond.

Jarred knew everything, every time Olivia texted me to say happy birthday or wish me a happy holiday, and every time someone hit on us while on leave when I couldn't even consider entertaining them. Olivia was my soul mate, the only person I ever considered myself with, and Jarred knew that and wanted that for me.

I continue reading the letter as confirmation that I didn't just dream all of this up and my best friend was waiting overseas for me to hear everything that's happened while home.

There is something I need you to do. I need you to do it for me, but it's also for you. You have a family, friends, people who love you and care about you do not lose them. You are my family, the only family that I have ever had, really. Which means I know you, I know you haven't been truly happy since Olivia and you're hoping every letter, every call is her. You're pushing everyone who loves you away.

I also know you are trying to deny this in your head, so stop.

I need you to get out. Retire. Go home. And find your happiness again.

I know what it's like to be unhappy and alone. That is not the life I want for my only brother. Don't make me fight you in a bar when we meet again.

Reading that last line again and again.

Every time it puts a hole in my heart.

Chapter 23

OLIVIA

Leaving home is always a challenge for me, especially when everyone is together because it doesn't happen often where the whole family is together, aside from Christmas. Plus, the boys are growing like weeds and I swear they are entirely different humans every time I see them.

Penelope and the boys are staying for another week, Cole and Carter live here so I'm having a little FOMO about leaving.

I drag my travel bag and work backpack down the stairs to pack my car and head back to the city. I only live two hours away from home and have a car that I use in Milwaukee, but it's an old beater Ford Focus that has been handed down through all of my siblings to me. I could buy a new car and finally get rid of the old girl but it still gets me from point A to point B safely and promptly, and is mostly reliable.

I would stay if I didn't have to work tomorrow but I volunteered to do so, and as the only physical therapist there, I'll have everyone's patients. I have a sense of obligation to maintain continuity of care to help the patients in the best way I can.

But there is still a heavy feeling associated with leaving today, one that I don't normally feel or experience.

I know everyone always says they have a magnetic connection with their person, I mean, that's the whole point of being with someone, right? You want your partner to be your best friend, to listen to you, to understand, to support you, to love you unconditionally. I have always felt it was a cliché, something that doesn't truly happen.

But as I'm packing the car to leave for the city, it feels wrong. I have an endless feeling of longing, of not getting closure with Noah, and an everlasting sensation to be near him again.

Damn it, I'm now wondering where he is and what he is doing today.

I know I never give myself enough time after a trip to settle and get prepared for the week ahead of me but what can two additional hours at home hurt? Fuck it. Let's pack the car and head to his house to see him one last time before heading back to the city.

He may be living back in Fisher Creek, but that doesn't mean I'm ever truly going to see him again anyway. A few more hours can't hurt.

I finish loading my car quickly and efficiently, making sure I have everything I need and the boys haven't hidden anything in my suitcase. The last time I saw them, they hid a favorite stuffed animal in my bag so I wouldn't feel lonely and would think about them often. Which turned into a panicked Penelope when the stuffy was missing and no one could find it anywhere.

I say a quick goodbye to everyone, promising to come back more often, knowing that probably won't happen. But there's something about saying "see ya later" to Pen that feels different. She pulls me into a deep hug and whispers, "see ya later, gator" into my ear, a cute sentiment we used to say to each other when she left for college. I make a mental note to schedule more calls and FaceTime with her, but right now I need to leave before I cry and never get out of here.

The drive from my house to Noah's would be a straight shot across town if there were a road that traveled straight through the woods. Instead, there is a winding road that lines a small river through the outskirts of town. Once you get to the center of town, it's a straight shot with about two turns to get to his long snow-covered driveway. Thankfully it hasn't been warm enough for any melting and refreezing to occur so getting to the house poses no problems, aside from having to drive slower than I'd like.

I'm so quick to get out of my car and run up the deck stairs that I don't notice the thin layer of ice coating the top of the deck until I'm already lying face down. Full of embarrassment, I look up as I see Noah's mom running out the front door. I jump up as quickly as I can without going down for a second time.

"I'm okay, I promise. Just clumsy" I stammer out, trying to assure her that it's only my pride that's hurt. It's not the first ice patch I have slipped on and will certainly not be the last, considering I live in Wisconsin.

"Is Noah here? I wanted to see him again quickly before heading back to the city," I say, changing the subject.

"Oh, honey, you just missed him. He left for his house," Ms. Kneland says, gripping my forearms.

"His house?" I ask, confused because he never told me he has a house in Fisher Creek or wherever it is. Why didn't we meet there the other day? Buying a house is a huge deal, and I feel like that is something you tell someone.

"He just got the keys this morning. It needs some TLC but he says the master just needs a fresh coat of paint before it'll be ready. I imagine that's what he's doing now," she says.

I must be in shock because I don't say anything in return.

"It's over on Tailer Road, you'll see the car when you get over there. Go see him, Olivia," she finishes.

Tailer Road is back by my parents' farm, and I think there's only one house over there for sale. Why did he buy a house that needs so much work? Before she has to tell me again, I turn on my heels and practically run down the stairs. I can hear her proud mama chuckle as I climb into the car and try not to peel out of the driveway.

I can't explain why but there's a deep part of me that needs to see Noah again.

And that is exactly what I'm going to do.

Chapter 24

NOAH

I'm just about finished taping the master bedroom and bathroom when I hear a knock on the front door. This is ridiculous because the only person who knows I'm here is my mom. And the house sits too far back from the road for anyone to see the car and Mom wouldn't knock, she would just walk in. Instead of going to investigate, I choose to ignore the noise and start opening up the can of paint I bought on the way here. I've decided that I'm painting the walls a light blue-gray color, but first I have to prime the obnoxiously red walls. Once the walls are primed, I can take my time doing the rest of the work.

I open the primer but before I can start to pour it, I hear the knock again. Okay, someone is here and I need to go see who it is and figure out why they are here. The master bedroom is the furthest room from the front door, overlooking the back of the property, but as you walk down the hallway toward the secondary hallway leading to the front door, you can see out the big window in the kitchen. The old Bennett family car is in my driveway.

Even more confused, I open the front door and feel the change in my facial expression. I'm utterly baffled to see Ollie standing on the front porch of my new house. She looks up at me with a small smile and is rocking back and forth, almost jittery like she's either freezing or extremely nervous to be here.

"Hi," she almost whispers with a small wave in front of her body.

"Ollie, hi, what are you doing here?" I finally get out of my shock and move into pure excitement and happiness.

"I needed to see you again before leaving," she replies, cheeks reddening with what appears to be embarrassment. "I know I said I had to get back to the city but I just really needed to see you. I went to your mom's house and she told me you were here."

I have no words. I'm in pure shock.

"Okay," I finally respond. "Come in," I say, opening the door into my house. I'm instantly aware of how dusty and old this house is.

There's an awkward silence that fills the air as we stand in the hallway between the empty family room and the empty dining room.

"You bought the Kinney property," she finally says.

"Yeah," I reply. "I didn't spend any money while in the Army, and after two weeks with Mom and Bec, I don't know how much longer I can survive."

"Fair. I couldn't ever live with my family again, but why a house that needs so much work?" she asks, sounding genuinely curious.

Ollie requires honesty, especially if I want to keep her in my life but I'm not sure I'm ready to talk about everything that happened overseas, or Jarred, especially with Ollie.

"I have a lot of free time, with only three shifts a week at the firehouse. Unless we get a call, and you know how often that happens," I start "I can't just sit around with my thoughts and feelings. So I bought a house that I can devote my time to making it mine," I finish.

Perfect. A half-truth.

"Oh," Ollie replies, sounding concerned. "Ya know, sometimes, thoughts and feelings are important to recognize and accept in order to heal," she says. Leave it to Ollie, to not directly ask what happened, but know that it's something significant and still have a statement that my therapist has said to me at least once a week since we started our sessions.

I know at this moment that I need to tell Ollie why I retired, what happened, and why I need the distraction. This beautiful woman has only been back in my life for less than a week and she has shown her selflessness has never changed. She has the biggest heart of anyone I know and always wants to ensure the safety and care of those around her.

"Let's take a tour of the house," I say softly, grabbing her hand to lead her through the house. She smiles softly and follows as I show her all the empty rooms and tell her about all of the changes and renovations I'm preparing to do. We finally make our way into the master bedroom where there is a big duffel bag with clothes, towels, and the contents of my desk. There's plastic lining the floor in front of two of the wall with the tin of paint and roller sitting right at the edge of the plastic.

"This is the master bedroom, I'm painting it a light gray because I want to keep it light with the big natural light from the back," I say as I realize I'm still holding her hand, I turn to face her and we are standing in the middle of the room, closer to the backside.

I let go of Ollie's hand as she walks closer to the windows, eyes wide, a smile building on her face.

"I love it," she says. "All of it, it's going to be perfect, Noah. Even with all the work you have to put in." I feel my shoulders sink again as

I look down to my feet getting ready to share what feels like one of my biggest secrets with Olivia.

"What?" She notices the change in my demeanor. "Noah, what is it?" she asks again with more nervousness than before.

My hands start to shake slightly and I clasp them together to keep her from noticing. This is silly, this shouldn't be that hard to tell her. I love Jarred, loved him with every ounce of my being, and she is going through something similar. So why does it feel like the air is being pulled out of my lungs?

"I am trying to find the words," I mumble, willing the shaking to stop and my heart to slow down.

"I know it has been a while but you can tell me anything," she says taking my hands in hers.

"Yeah, thanks," I barely get it out, trying to find the best way to tell her that I've been rebuilding my entire life for the last six months. That I watched my best friend die, in front of me while saving me and the rest of our unit. How do I ease into that?

"Just tell me Noah, it's not like you are married or something, is it?" she responds, with an obvious hint of frustration. "You're not married are you?" she asks urgently.

"What? No! Ollie, of course I'm not married." I pull my hands out of her grip and create some space between us. Space that I hope will get air into my collapsing airway, and light from the bright windows pushes the darkness associated with the memory away.

She doesn't say anything, she simply just stares at me, eyes narrowing with a mix of frustration and confusion, emotions pulsing through her like a current. I take a deep breath and hang my head low, still fighting for my bearings, knowing that Dr. Doyle would be happy to know that I finally was able to tell someone outside of my immediate family.

"Ollie, my best friend was killed. We were ambushed and a lot of people were lost that day," I struggle to blurt out.

"Oh, Noah..." Ollie starts as she takes a step closer to me, bringing her hands onto my forearms.

"After that day, I went into a very dark place. There was a lot of alcohol and I was a shell of a human until I started to see Dr. Doyle. It took four months to dig out of that hole. That's why I need this house. I need this as a coping mechanism when things are hard," I say, knowing that if I don't say it right away, I won't. And this is also part of Dr. Doyle's recovery plan, getting to a point where I can talk about Jarred.

Jarred, the 6 foot 4 giant teddy bear of a man that I got to call my best friend. He was the friend who was always laughing, joking, trying to make everyone around him have a good time, even when he wasn't. His hazel eyes and cooked smile never quite fit the intensity of his physique. He was built like a tight end with tattoos coating his left arm and entire back. But what really stood out about Jarred was his personality, his kind heart, taking a chance on everyone around him even though no one took a chance on him.

"Hey, what are you thinking about right now? Where did you go there?" I hear Ollie's voice and feel the touch of her hands on my forearms, bringing me out of the memories of my best friend.

"Sorry, I was thinking about Jarred, even just thinking about him here makes my heart hurt. I feel an indescribable pain in my chest, where I feel like all of my insides are falling out of me, and there isn't a bandage, or tourniquet that could keep them in. It wasn't until Jarred, that I realized you can have soul friends. The friends who are your soulmates, except just friends. The friends that you don't have to talk to all day everyday, but they get you and just being with them is enough. They can read you like a book even when you don't want them to and push you to do the hard things. The things you would never choose to do yourself. Jarred is that for me. *Was.* Was that for me." I stumble over the last sentence, still struggling to process that he is gone.

"I'm sorry, Noah. I know that doesn't change anything, but I'm sorry," she says, pulling me into an embrace. Ollie is small, but mighty, and while my head stands square over her I lower my forehead to the top of hers and soak in this moment. I'm so caught up in the moment that I don't realize we've moved onto the plastic near the tin of paint.

"But you got this house and have incredible plans for it, and painting while sad is not nearly as fun or effective," Ollie says with a smirk on her face as she pulls away from our hug and in one swift motion dips her hand in the tin of paint and wipes it across the side of my face and cheek.

Shocked by a smile, and the newly white paint smeared across the side of my face, I can't decide whether or not to be annoyed or laugh.

"I hope you don't like what you're wearing." I grin and laugh as I look at her black leggings and white cropped sweatshirt that are now speckled with white paint.

Ollie gasps and laughs all at once before dipping her hand in the paint and placing it squarely on my chest. Instinctively, I place my hand around her waist and pull her into my chest. Olivia squeaks with surprise and takes her opposite hand to wrap around my neck as we spin in a circle.

"There is the laugh that I love so much," I say, smiling. Her laugh is loud and deep but entirely infectious. She can bring anyone out of a bad mood, even if just for a moment with her laugh.

"There is the person who brings it out me," she replies as we come to a stop she looks up and leans in so that her lips meet mine, and I know I'm a goner.

Chapter 25

OLIVIA

S hit, did I just tell him that he's the only reason I laugh. How pathetic does that sound? Why would I say something like that?

I try to refocus on the scene around me. This house is old, but beautiful in the weirdest way. The wood floors are original and in immaculate condition, aside from some needing a quick sweep. I swear there used to be carpet throughout the living room and two bedrooms but it must've been ripped up. I never understood why people put wall-to-wall carpet in houses that have the perfect wooden floors.

Now we're standing here in his unpainted master bedroom, covered in white paint, intertwined with each other. This is not what friends do. Friends help each other paint, get food for one another, listen to the stories and the pain. Friends do not,bury their heads into each other, kiss each other deeply, passionately, and full of love.

Noah led me throughout his new house describing all of the changes he's looking to make over the next few months, and I could feel his excitement and eagerness to complete the project. It brings a smile to my face that I don't even try to hide because I couldn't be more proud of him. He's doing the hard work to create the best life for him after the Army.

As we got toward the back of the house I feel my body start to tense, my body temperature rising and the butterflies start swarming in my abdomen. I was so nervous walking into Noah's bedroom, afraid of making the same mistake we made a few nights ago. Okay, not that hooking up with Noah was a mistake because it was amazing but I live over two hours away and it doesn't make sense to get attached again. It would be pointless to fall back in love with this man who broke my heart but just as quickly put it back together.

However, hearing the hurt in his voice about Jarred and what happened made it more clear that this was exactly where I needed to be. Despite everything that's happened between Noah and me, no one should go through heartache, loss, and grief alone especially the type of loss that Noah experienced.

His best friend was killed in the line of duty, essentially right in front of him.

I can't even fathom what that must feel like, the sadness, the anger, potential guilt, and all the additional emotions that are tied to that kind of struggle.

But between the two of us, Noah has always been the sunshiney one, the happy-go-lucky, outgoing golden retriever that everyone knows and loves. He's known for picking everyone up when they are down, literally everyone.

He once picked up another player on the rival soccer team after we won the state championship game. He never lets anyone suffer or drown in their feelings alone.

Yet, here, talking about Jarred, his shoulders sunk, his head pointed toward the floor, and when he finally looks at me his eyes began to water. He's put in a lot of work to get to the point where he can talk about what happened so I have to return him the same kindness that he has given everyone over the years.

Trying to find the best way to take Noah by surprise but also make him laugh is not going to be an easy task. We're in an empty house, aside from a tin of paint. Taking in my surroundings, I realize I have a total of two options, either kiss Noah or splash him with the white paint on the floor.

There is a part of me deep down that wants nothing more than to reach up, and bring his soft lips to mine once again but I settle on the latter. I have one opportunity to do this, to get the paint and Noah without ruining the floor. I've always been incredibly clumsy so I need to time it perfectly. I need to be quick but swift, like a shadow.

Easy. Pull him close, use our connection as a distraction as we slide over toward the plastic, and as I pull my head away from his chest, leaving one arm on his forearm, I sweep my free hand into the tin of paint and quickly place a handprint on the side of Noah's face.

He gasps.

Audibly.

I know immediately I've made the right choice. His jaw is left hanging open from the shock but quickly turns into a devious smirk as he proceeds to splatter me back. Thankfully, I'm wearing my old worn out travel pants, so being covered in paint is not a problem.

Without even thinking I lean up and kiss Noah hard as if the world is ending and this is the last kiss I'll ever have. His lips are soft and welcoming, but I can also feel his initial shock. I want to run my hands all over his body but settle for placing one on his chest, the other grabbing the bottom of his shirt.

He kisses me back, full of desire and need, placing one hand on the small of my back, and the other firmly on my ass, pulling me closer and kissing me deeper. His hand moves so they are both under me and lifting me to his chest. I wrap my legs around him, laughing as he places a kiss at the nape of my neck as we walk across the room toward the wall and the big windows overlooking the backyard. This man is good at multitasking and knows all the right spots.

By the time he puts me down, I can't handle it anymore. I need more. More of Noah and his body. I'm pulling at the bottom of his shirt wanting it off. Now.

His smirk turns devilish as he tears the shirt off over his head and starts at mine. My sweatshirt is off in a matter of seconds, exposing my burgundy lace bralette above my high-waisted yoga pants. I reach for his belt and jeans, wondering why this man never wears comfy clothes.

We have hooked up twice since I've been home and I still haven't taken a moment to really look at his beautiful dick. Spinning so his back is to the wall, I drop to my knees, slowly gripping his dick at its base, taking it all in. He leans against the wall, head back, with one hand in my hair and the other on the top of his head. I smirk knowing he has completely lost control and I'm going to fully unravel him.

"Fuck, Ollie," he bites out with a bit of a moan. "You haven't even started yet and I can feel the tension building."

Without saying a word, I slide his dick into my mouth, swirling my tongue across it, looking up as I take every inch.

"You look amazing with your pretty little lips wrapped around my cock," he says, regaining control and taking command of the moment.

Releasing him I smirk and say, "I want you to fuck my mouth until I choke..."

Before I can finish that sentence, he slams his hips forward as deep as he can go, and I feel the build-up in his body, his muscles tensing from pleasure and he begins to reach climax. Right when I think he's about to let it all go and let me get a full taste of him, he pulls out entirely, drops in front of me and pushes me onto my back.

"I'm not finishing until you are good and satisfied, baby," he says, planting a kiss on my neck and sliding his hands to the band of my pants, sliding them down over my ass and throwing them across the room.

He looks down at my pussy with a deep hunger in his eyes.

"I bet you're already wet for me," he says as he slides between my knees pressing his finger against my clit. I shake my head yes in reply waiting for his next moves but the pressure of his finger has me already writhing my hips.

"I knew you would be."

Noah slides his tongue up my slit and sucks on my clit in a way I didn't know was possible. This perfect pattern of licking and sucking that keeps me on the edge of wanting more. He curls his finger inside me to find the exact spot to send me into oblivion but he only keeps it there for a minute, giving me the pleasure I so desperately want, but taking it away an instant later.

"I swear to God, if you do not fuck me right now. I am going to walk to my car, get my vibrator, and show you how it's done myself," I growl, after the fifth time.

He just chuckles, coming up for air, and smirking at me.

"That sounds like a fun time, but I want to feel you come around my cock, so you're staying right where you are."

Stubborn as a mule and determined to no longer wait another second I start to prop myself up to leave when I am met with large hands and broad shoulders pushing me back down, tearing my arms out from under me. My hands are slid from my sides up over my head and held in place. His big brooding chest is above mine, staring down at me.

"I told you to stay where you are." My entire body quivers at his new dominating tone. It's hot. I have never seen Noah be so stern and in charge and it makes me wonder what would happen if I disobey him again.

Not moving his hands from my wrists, he slides my knees wider and uses his free hand to bend one up onto his shoulder before sliding his dick against my entrance. I audibly whimper in anticipation, need, desire.

I fucking whimper but before I have the time to think too much about it, he plows into me.

"Shit, Noah, I'm close," I moan, closing my eyes.

"Good, I don't think I can last much longer with your tight pussy clenching around me. Let go, Ollie, come all over my dick," he says as he pinches my clit one final time sending me over the edge, taking him with me.

♪ ♪ ♪

Lying in a pile of arms and legs on the floor with Noah was not on the agenda for today, and I'm supposed to be back in Milwaukee already. Caroline and Mason are going to be waiting for all the details. I can't help but roll my eyes and smile thinking about my friends and how they'll not only want the details but all the juicy bits after they question me why I'm at least six hours later than I originally planned.

I know I need to leave, but this feels right. It feels like the part of me that has been lost and shoved deep down inside me is finally at peace. I want more time with Noah, not knowing when I'll get this time again.

"Ollie," he says quietly. There's something about the way he says it that tells me he's going to say something I don't want to hear.

"No," I say quickly. "Noah, we don't have to talk about it. I'm going back to Milwaukee today and you're going to be here. There's no point in adding more to it," I finish, my voice cracking a little at the end.

He just nods, not saying anything, and rolls to wrap me in a hug. A hug that feels empty, feels like goodbye.

I shiver, partly because it's chilly, but mostly because this sucks. The feeling of the walls closing in, trapping me, and taking out everyone I care about sitting like a black hole in my diaphragm. Noah notices my shiver, and thinking I'm cold quickly hands me my sweatshirt and leggings to warm me up.

Little does he know there's a part of me that's breaking all over again.

Looking out the window, the sun is shining bright and high in the sky. My stomach grumbles and I quickly place my hand over my abdomen, as if that'll silence the noise. It has to be around lunchtime and I didn't eat breakfast this morning in a rush to leave.

Noah, shimmying into his jeans, glances over at me, and I feel my face heat with a little embarrassment as he asks, "Ollie, did you eat breakfast today?"

"No, I rushed out of the house to see you," I reply, with a hint of spice to my tone. Knowing full well he is about to call me out for not eating breakfast, because it's a well-known fact that I'm a monster when I don't eat. Which is why I always have some sort of breakfast packed for when I arrive at the office in the morning.

"Ollie," he says with that disapproving stern mom look he does so well.

"I know. I know. I ..." I interrupt before he takes me by the arm and walks me back out into the kitchen. He places me on the counter next to the fridge. He opens it and he hands me my favorite flavor of seltzer water, strawberry lemon, and pulls out a throw-away tin with an aluminum foil cover on it.

"Mom gave me food this morning to bring over for today and tomorrow," he says, continuing to pull out the dishes, utensil and quickly heats what looks like a five-layer homemade lasagna. I can feel my mouth begin to water just looking at it.

We eat in almost silence, except for the slight noise of forks clinking on the plates and the occasional chewing sound. I jump up to start cleaning once we finish, bringing the dishes over to the sink.

"You don't need to do that," he says as I turn on the water.

"You cook, I clean," I say in response. "Plus, I really don't mind. Let me finish this and then we'll paint the bedroom to get you caught up for today's renovations," I finish with a smirk.

He just shakes his head back and forth and heads back down the long hallway toward the bedroom to get everything ready to start. The least I can do is help him by cleaning the dishes and painting the bedroom since he fed me and I distracted him from renovations for a few hours. Plus, I need more time. My heart needs a few more hours with Noah.

We paint the entire bedroom in just under two hours and it looks like an entirely different room in the best way. Once we clean up the plastic, wash the paint brushes, and do a final sweep of the floor in the room I know it's time for me to head back to the city. Time to say goodbye for now.

Noah walks me outside to my car and the driveway is starting to get mushy from the high sun we have had all day. Turning to face him, I feel my eyes start to water as I fight my bottom lip from quivering. I will not cry. Not in front of him today.

I've had a great week at home with him but our lives are in different places. I have my life and my career in Milwaukee. He's starting his life here in Fisher Creek. There's too much distance, too much hurt, and too many what-ifs to start this again. It's not fair to Noah or myself, and therefore he doesn't get to see how much this trip has affected me.

He takes me into a hug and kisses the top of my head and we stand in silence for a moment before I get into my car and pull out of the driveway. Looking in the rearview mirror, I see Noah standing there, hands in his pockets, looking down at the ground. The snow piles surrounding him slowly engulf him as I begin to cry.

And I cry the entire way to Milwaukee.

Chapter 26

OLIVIA

It's been two weeks since I left Fisher Creek. Two weeks since I had that final kiss with Noah and we painted his bedroom.

In those two weeks, I haven't talked to him at all. I'm not naive enough to think he doesn't want to talk to me, but I'm too stubborn to call him myself. That being said, there is not a single day that he doesn't cross my mind, which is decidedly annoying.

The first week back, I was the only physical therapist in the office and we had a full schedule. I had a new patient who works with the Milwaukee EMS come in for an appointment following a job injury which typically would send me into a tizzy about Cole, but this time it was Noah. I understand being a firefighter is an intense occupation. I understand being in the Army is probably more intense and injuries happen but that doesn't mean I have to like it.

Being that we are the primary office for all first responders, fire-fighters, and police officers in Milwaukee, this is a normal occurrence for me, which typically ends with me dialing Cole on lunch to check in.

"Hey, Liv," he says, out of breath when he finally answers on the fourth ring.

"Hey, sorry, good time?" I ask, instantly regretting bugging him during the day.

"Always a good time for the baby sis," he responds, and my frown turns into a small smile.

"I don't have a lot of time, it's lunch, but I just wanted to check in and make sure everyone is okay?" I ask hesitantly.

Something crashes behind him, followed by laughter and another bang. I instantly freeze. I know that laugh. Noah. Why is Cole hanging out with Noah in the middle of the day? They haven't been friends in years. He must be at the station with the guys, screwing around per usual. I roll my eyes listening to Cole yell "hey" at the guys followed by a soft chuckle.

"Yeah, Liv, everyone is fine. Why?" he asks suspiciously.

"EMS patient, sorry to bother you. Bye," I say, feeling like the annoying little sister who wants to be included in everything.

"Wait," he says with a sigh. We've had this conversation at least fifteen times before and he knows that treating injured emergency personnel always worries me. I don't hang up but also don't say anything in response. I hear a door close and know he's walked into the office for some privacy.

"Liv, I know treating emergency personnel can be hard for you and that you immediately think of me but, I promise you we are good and safe," he says reassuringly.

We? Who are "we"? And why does he think I'm concerned about anyone else?

"Thanks, Cole. I just needed to check-in. This was a rough one. Hey, I gotta get back to the office, talk soon."

"Love ya, Liv," he says before hanging up.

I feel a combination of stupid and annoying, but also a sense of relief. Fisher Creek is an extremely small town, where not a lot of big emergencies happen, but accidents still happen. Thunderstorms still knock down trees. Teenagers still make stupid decisions. Emergencies happen. I can't help but worry now and again.

Later that night, is the first time I consider calling Noah. After a long day, a night bath and a glass of wine, I'm now laying in bed staring at Noah's contact. My inner monologue weighs the pros and cons of calling him for at least thirty minutes before I decide against it.

Thinking about Noah is all-consuming, I'm not sleeping, I'm barely surviving work, and I don't want to do anything. Remembering the nights we've shared, the kisses, and the magnetism between us is affecting all aspects of my life.

Caroline and I are fighting more often and I know it's because I'm being a colossal bitch. I'm grumpy and I don't want to go out to the bars and I definitely don't want to go on double dates. I just really haven't been myself. I make a promise to myself to be better for my friends because I know they have been the best to me.

Waking up after yet another night with almost no sleep, I have a headache, my eyes feel heavy, and I'm in dire need of caffeine before attempting to get my day together. It's Saturday and I want to go for a run this morning to try to clear my head and get out of this funk before Caroline and I head to the bookstore. Then later this evening we are meeting Mason and Savannah for drinks.

Throwing on whatever comfy sweats I can find with my sports bra, I put my hair into the messiest bun and look for my big glasses before stumbling into the kitchen for some coffee.

Standing in the kitchen, I notice a note from Caroline on the counter that reads.

Got called into the studio for an emergent story this morning. Bookstore tomorrow?

I'm not surprised, but a little disappointed, because today's supposed to be the day everything goes back to normal for us. Caroline has been my best friend and rock for the last nine years. Our friendship is so important to me and I want to make sure I nurture our friendship the way it deserves. I also understand that Caroline has been picking up as many extra shifts as possible after breaking up with Ben over the holidays.

She says it was just one of those things where things were good, but not great. She was happy, but felt like they weren't constantly having fun. That he couldn't be her best friend and would settle for where they were in life instead of pushing her to be the best.

I startle at the knock on the door because I'm not expecting anyone. Caroline's at work and Mason and Savannah are traveling home from Chicago today, not expected to be back until later this afternoon, and none of them would knock.

The knocking continues as I'm too busy thinking to even move to see who it is. I have watched too many crime shows and read too many thrillers to just open the door empty-handed. Grabbing the biggest knife from the block and hiding it behind my back, I walk over to the front door.

At this point, I'm standing on the other side of the door when whoever is there knocks again, this time a little more firm and aggressive.

"Cole?" I say, looking through the peephole. I quickly unlock the door and open it. "What the heck are you doing here?" I ask as Cole pushes through the front door.

"We missed ya and wanted to go out in the city," he says slyly.

"We?" I question.

"Yes, we, Ollie," Noah says as he walks through the front door into the living room.

And I melt.

Chapter 27

NOAH

"Jesus, Olivia, what's with the butcher knife?" Cole shouts as she drops her arms at her side in shock after I walk into her house. Surprising, Olivia in Milwaukee has gone about as I expected. She's both surprised in the best way and angry that we didn't warn her so she could clean the entire house in preparation.

"Well, I wasn't expecting anyone and I wasn't about to get murdered in my own house," she says as she recuperates and places the knife flat on the counter.

I can't help but laugh, because imagining the tiny five-foot-five Ollie stabbing someone is just so far out of her character.

Cole plops onto the couch like he owns the place, and Ollie returns to the kitchen where she left her cup of coffee on the white granite countertop. Pulling two other coffee mugs out of the dark gray cabinets above the three different types of coffee makers. Who needs that many different coffee makers? Are there even that many different types of coffee?

"Do you guys want coffee? Caroline made a pot this morning, it's still hot," Ollie offers. "Noah, you can sit down, you don't have to stand by the door," she adds, looking up from her mug.

Cole chuckles to himself at my awkwardness of just standing here and motions for me to come over and sit down.

I have never been this awkward with Ollie before, we've always been so comfortable with each other. So why am I being weird now? Because Cole is here? That was never the issue in high school. Plus, after Christmas, when Ollie returned to Milwaukee, I went on a bit of a bender, spending most of my free time at Fishy's or killing myself at the station gym.

Cole found me one night after a few too many beers, trying to run off the drunk on the treadmill at the station. He asked me if I was trying to kill myself, and then made me stop, sit down, and tell him what was going on.

So I did. I told him exactly what happened in Oklahoma, and why I did what I did. I told him about Jarred and showed him the letter. I told him about the first night with Ollie, the Christmas Eve party, imagining a future with Ollie, and the paint party.

But most importantly that I'm still in love with Ollie and I haven't been able to get her out of my mind since she left.

After telling him everything, I expected Cole to punch me in the face. Ollie's his little sister, and that was the deal. If I ever hurt Ollie, I was getting punched. Instead, he climbed out of his chair and fully embraced me. Cole is one of the best guys I know, he is supportive, protective, and understanding.

He told me that if I truly loved Ollie then I shouldn't let her get away.

That was the first night Cole had truly spoken to me in years and he continues to show that kindness and support he always had, and for that, I'm eternally grateful. Heck, it was his idea to come to Milwaukee in the first place, and also his idea not to tell Ollie we were coming. Seeing the happy shock on her face was so worth it. It's like a little light turned on inside of her.

After talking to Cole that night we started training together, running a few miles in the morning, lifting during our shift at the station, and since it's slow at the farm, he comes over most nights with some beer to help with the renovations.

I didn't realize that Cole made a point to visit Ollie a few times a year, so when Caroline texted to say she's in a slump and wasn't even attempting to pull herself out of it, he knew he had to go sooner rather than later.

"How are the renovations?" Ollie asks as she hands Cole his coffee and settles in a cozy Sherpa chair, wrapping a knit blanket around her legs.

"Great, Cole has been helping out a few nights a week. We're working on the kitchen now," I say, wishing I had taken some photos to show her.

"Liv, Noah wants you to show him around the city today. Where are Caroline and Mason?" Cole interrupts the conversation. As much as he's trying to hide it, he's definitely pushing for us to have some alone time to talk through our past and rekindle this friendship further. He wants to spend some uninterrupted time with Caroline too.

"Caroline got called into the studio to cover a story this morning but should be home around three. Mason and Savy are coming home today. We are all supposed to get drinks down at the pub a couple blocks over around six. So we have most of the day to explore. Cole, anywhere in particular you want to go?" Ollie asks, with a plethora of emotions disappointment that Caroline is working, and excitement to explore the city. They hit like a wave rushing through her all at once.

"No, I had a late night at the station last night. I'm going to stay in and take a nap so we can rave at the bar tonight," he responds, kicking his feet up on the couch and pulling a blanket over himself.

"Are you sure? You love the waterfront with all the food stands."

Cole doesn't even bother to respond but instead closes his eyes and pretends to snore loudly.

I can't help but roll my eyes at him and chuckle before turning to Ollie.

"Let's start at the bookstore," I say with a slight smirk on my face. I know that Ollie has at least three bookstores she frequents, and it's probably her favorite place to be outside of her reading nook. "I need a new book or two," I finish, almost forgetting that Ollie is the only one who knows I love a good book.

The look on Cole's face is full of confusion when he finally opens his eyes.

Chapter 28

OLIVIA

I quickly text Caroline as I get ready for the day. The goal is to change into something cute but comfy, that looks nice but also not like I'm trying too hard. It's just Noah, this man has seen me through the thick of my high school phase. So why it matters now, I really don't know.

Caroline and I go to a bookstore together once a month, picking out some new books, one we both get, one the other recommends, and one we want to read ourselves to share throughout the month. We alternate stores because there are so many great ones here, including both new and used bookstores. I have to show Noah the best, which means either Boswell or Voyageur, and it's impossible to pick between the two.

She replies moments later.

Caroline loves Voyageur, mostly because she can pick out books while petting and hanging out with the store cats. Whereas, I don't care much for the cat snuggles and would rather pick out a good book. Caroline and I haven't talked much about Noah since the day I got back from Fisher Creek, and I don't know how to tell her he is here. At least Cole is here and I can pawn them off each other on that.

> **Me: Cole & Noah are here. Noah wants a city tour before drinks today and requested the first stop - my FAVORITE bookstore.**

I add a wide eye emoji to the end of that.

> **Caroline: Cole is here??????????**

> **Caroline: And Noah?**

> **Caroline: Since when? Why?**

She immediately types back, each message individual in rapid fire. Caroline has always had a soft spot for Cole, and we love all hanging out together when he is in town. But I can't help but wonder if there's anything going on between the two of them. They are each a little squirrely around the other.

> **Me: No clue, but honestly not complaining. Still on for drinks tonight?**

> **Caroline: Abso-fucking-lutely**

She replies with a smile and a glass of brown liquid symbolizing a bourbon glass emoji. She must be having a heck of a day at work. I start to wonder what kind of catastrophe she is witnessing today to warrant that type of response. Being a journalist in a large city, with the primary role of covering breaking news must actually be exhausting.

I pull out an oversized cream-colored cable knit button-up sweater to wear over a tank top and leggings. I have thicker mid-calf height socks and Blundstone boots on trying to brave the cold. Living in the city is a blast but the best way to do a tour of our favorite places is walking which means layers, layers, layers. My dark gray mid-thigh length puffer coat is less than flattering but does a great job at blocking out the wind while walking through downtown.

Since Cole decided to bail on our city tour, probably to allow us some quality "catching up time", please let my eyes roll harder at him next time. I want to be strategic on tour stops. We can't go anywhere alone, I cannot be trusted alone with the faint upward curl of his lips, or the perfect wave to his dark brown hair that I want to sink my hands back into.

Okay, I need to stop. It's only been two weeks since I touched him last and I'm acting like it has been a century and he's not even mine to touch.

Boswell is usually jam-packed on a Saturday afternoon, especially in January. So naturally the day I want it to be busy happens to be the one day and hour there's no one inside.

Bernadette, the store manager, gives me a smile and a quick wave as we walk through the old heavy door, which is my sign that I might spend too much time here.

Noah has never fully admitted to everyone that he loves books, but it's also always been clear by the way he stands taller and the small thin smile that creeps along his face that he is obsessed. Truthfully, he was a popular, annoying, jock in high school and I imagine that having a secret love for books, of all genres might I add, would hurt his reputation so he kept it on the down low.

I probably would never have known his secret if Cole and I hadn't tried to surprise him the day after his dad passed with cookies and coffee, and found him sitting on the back deck of his house nose-deep in a fantasy book.

Boswell is an old brick building, with an open concept inside and four distinct rooms that have wall-to-wall bookshelves and a few tables scattered throughout the middle. Each room is dedicated to a different genre with romance and fantasy being the largest found on opposite sides of the building. Presumably to ensure you walk through the entire store to explore the most popular sections, which is a brilliant marketing move that never fails to get me every time.

When we first enter the building I head to the romance section, in dire need of a cheesy, and spicy palate-cleansing romance read, and Noah heads to the fantasy section after talking about a new fantasy author I've never heard of. There is a super distinct smell associated with buying new books, similar to that new car smell everyone loves. Me, I'm obsessed with the smell of the bookstore.

The dry earthy scent of the pages contrasts the brightly lit space from the large windows and the snow reflecting from the outside make this my little piece of heaven. I take my puffer jacket off and wrap it through the strap of my bag so I have free arms and hands for all the books I am about to engorge in. I find myself in front of the new release section, nose-deep in the new release from my favorite author, fully immersed in the smell and feel of holding it in my hand that I don't hear Noah walk up behind me until he places a hand on my shoulder.

Practically jumping out of my skin, I whirl around, ready to punch whoever is behind me when I realize it's Noah.

Realizing he startled me, and knowing my history as a klutz, he reaches out to catch me, resulting in his hands on either side of me against the shelf that I'm now leaning against, the book still in my hand, heart racing.

"Little jumpy, huh, Ollie?" he says with a smirk.

"You snuck up behind me out of nowhere!" I retort.

He chuckles and replies, "What are you reading there?"

I slam the book shut, feel my face heat, and stare at the closed book. Just because we had sex doesn't mean he needs to know the dirty scenes I love reading and fantasizing over.

"Wouldn't you like to know?" I say, trying to turn away from him. He's too quick, turning me back against the bookshelf and lifting my chin with his thumb, pressing closer to me. How the hell did he move so quickly? My core starts to heat, every neuron in my body firing, tingling with anticipation of his next move.

Brushing his thumb over my lower lip and leaning down, I can feel his breath against my neck when he whispers, "I want to know everything about you, especially what makes your heart race and legs shake."

He slowly traces his thumb across my bare collarbone, as my sweater slides off my shoulder, bringing his forehead against me, and my breath starts to labor.

"I am going to learn everything, to figure out exactly what you like."

His arm against the bookshelf is blocking my head from turning as he leans inward, I gasp, feeling his ice cold hand brush up against my abdomen approaching my already hard nipple.

The book I'm holding falls to one hand and hangs by my side as I loop my fingers into the waistband of his jeans, annoyed that they're locked into place by the belt he's wearing.

"Like the way you stop breathing when I do this," he starts, pinching my nipple enough to hurt in all the best ways. There's an ache, a need for more, as I tilt my head up to the ceiling, exposing my neck and waiting for the next touch.

When I close my eyes I can feel his lips hovering right over the sensitive part of my neck, giving my nipple another pinch taking my breath away when we hear, "Oh, honey, right this way, that book is on the small white table in the romance section."

Fuck.

Noah stands tall, removing his hand from underneath my shirt, draining the heat from my body with him. My face flushes, not with the desire, and lust that was just there but from a hint of fear and embarrassment at what we were doing *in public* and almost got caught.

"We can do what's in that book later. Let's get some food," Noah says, appearing utterly unfazed by everything that's just happened as he grabs my hand and leads me to the check-out counter.

Chapter 29

NOAH

"When you said we were going to 'the pub down the street' I didn't think its name was actually the Pub Down the Street," I say to Ollie as we walk up to the pub to see this lively redhead pipe up from a table in the back, waving us over.

Ollie just shrugs in response. I can feel her emotions shift as the biggest smile grows on her face. "That's Caroline," she says.

Looking back to the firecracker, I see Cole sitting at the table across from her, head down playing something on his phone. Caroline's excitement as she's jumping up and down waiting for us to come over is comical and I'm half surprised she hasn't run across the bar to hug Ollie as if she hasn't seen her in a month...when in reality they live together.

Cole stands up next to Caroline with a huge shit-eating grin on his face as we approach and I can't help but wonder what he did all day and if there is something secret going on between the two. Cole would vehemently deny it for Ollie's sake, but I don't think she would mind it. It's clear she has a deep connection and friendship with Caroline, and I've known both Ollie and Cole forever so there's no doubt about the connection they share.

"Are Mason and Savy here yet?" Ollie asks Caroline as we approach the table.

"No, they got stuck in traffic on 43," Caroline replies with an annoyed look on her face.

"Ugh, that's the worst highway coming into the city," Ollie replies.

We sit down across from Caroline and Cole, leaving space for the others at the end of the table when they get here.

"Caroline and I met at a spin class downtown," she tells me.

"Technically not originally. I did the new business piece when the practice opened." Caroline interjects. I learn that Caroline is a journalist and a bit of an adrenaline junkie so she always tries to report on the big events, controversial topics, and basically anything in between that people will talk about.

"Okay, fair, but we didn't become friends until Syd tried to kill us in our first spin class and we could barely walk out." Ollie laughs. Caroline and Ollie lean their heads together as they recount that moment and it is clear the love they have for each other.

I don't hear the initial comment Cole makes but I only assume it's full of snark based on the shared snarled look they share before Caroline retorts, "I don't know why you act like you hate this, you know you're one minute away from falling in love with me."

I almost spit out my beer, laughing at her remark.

Cole's face turns so red it matches the color of his ale and he rolls his eyes before looking back at his phone. At this moment I know Caroline is the person Cole has been keeping a secret.

As we start to round 11 p.m., everyone's getting tired and I'm grateful to be making the short trek back to the house. The time at the bar has solidified my notion that Ollie is exactly where she needs to be. The way she lights up when her friends are talking and how she's fully invested in listening and caring about what they have to say warms me from the inside out.

She's always been empathetic but strong in her belief system, and it's clear that after all her time in the city, and all of our problems that she never lost sight of it...and that might actually be the hottest thing about her. She stand by the people she loves, and show them the love and support that they need, even when their beliefs are different from her own. It draws me into Ollie more than ever.

It's probably a good thing that we had a few drinks tonight to give me some liquid courage to place my hand on the small of her back as we walk and then transition to putting it around her shoulder for the walk home.

Initially, she tenses for a moment as a bolt of electricity shoots through both of us, pulling me closer to her but quickly relaxes into my shoulder and makes the journey home tucked tightly into my side.

Where I wish she would stay forever.

While it's a short walk back to the house we make it two blocks before Ollie is pulled away by Caroline as they walk hand in hand, laughing and giggling the remainder of the walk home. I can't hide the smile that comes across my face as I watch them walk ahead, Ollie grabbing Savy's arm to join them. Mason and Cole fall back to walk with me and watch the three girls with giddy smiles on their faces.

"They're three peas in a pod," Cole says finally. He looks at Mason and continues "How the hell do you live with them all the time?"

Mason just chuckles and shrugs off the question before saying, "The way they just took Savannah in and made her one of us is something I will forever be grateful for."

It's clear he really cares about Savannah but also values his relationship with Ollie and Caroline. I mean, they have lived together for the last nine years so I really shouldn't be surprised.

Watching the three girls, they are all entirely different personalities that I couldn't imagine meshing together initially. Caroline's the firecracker, a wild child that goes perfectly with her vibrant red hair and her long ass legs. I swear they go on for miles. It's also the main part of Caroline that Cole cannot stop looking at. Whereas, Savannah is shorter than Ollie, with medium-length wavy blonde hair. She's the wallflower of the group. Ollie is the in-between of the two different girls.

As we climb the front stairs, Caroline fumbles with the lock, each girl pairing off with one of us. We barely make it into the living room before Mason and Savannah disappear up stairs. Caroline and Ollie grab an extra blanket and pillows for the couch from the closet where Cole and I are going to sleep. Thankfully they have a large sectional so there's plenty of space for each of us to sleep in our own space.

Once Caroline drags herself down the hallway to bed, Ollie tucks herself firmly into my chest, pressing the side of her face into my chest. I wrap my arms around her shoulders, pulling her tight to me, resting my chin on the top of her head. Cole just rolls over, making a gagging noise like he used to do back when we were teenagers even though we all know he's in full support of this, otherwise he wouldn't have brought me out here for his weekend getaway. I can feel Ollie smile in response to Cole and everything feels right. Like we're exactly where we're supposed to be.

"I should go to bed, we have a full day tomorrow before you leave," Ollie says in a muffled tone, still leaning against me. I know she is right but it's nearly impossible to hide the disappointment from having to let her go. I know she is still skeptical about our relationship and that is entirely my fault, but I just wish she would let me back in. At least give me a chance.

"Okay," I whisper in response, slowly loosening my grip. She pulls the top half of her off me placing both her hands on my chest with a slight sleepy smile on her face.

Fuck.

There is no way I'm going to be able to let her go when she looks at me like that. The look on her face as the corner of her mouth starts to curl up into the sexiest smirk tells me she's had too much to drink and knows exactly what that look does to me.

"Ollie, go to bed now, or Cole's going to hear the sounds you make when I kiss you," I say with both my hands on the small of her back, secretly hoping she decides to torture her brother.

She pulls away, without saying a word, clearly signifying this is not going in my favor tonight. Then before I even know what hit me she launches onto her tiptoes to give me a peck on the cheek before whispering "good night" and disappearing down the hallway to her bedroom.

I hear the soft chuckle of Cole who's pretending to be asleep on his side of the sectional. I am thankful we have been able to fall back into the friendship we've shared since we were five, as if that dreaded decade didn't exist.

Ugh. My entire body aches for Ollie as I crawl onto the couch under the knit blanket Ollie left for me. The ache deepens when I realize this is the same blanket we used on the porch swing all those years ago when I finally gave in to my feelings for her. I have never been a great sleeper but there is no way I'm going to sleep tonight now.

And I'm right. For the next three hours, I'm either tossing and turning or staring at the ceiling wondering if Ollie is asleep. I even get up twice and creep to the beginning of the hallway before stopping realizing I have no idea what room is hers and that is not a risk I'm willing to take. Plus, it's fairly clear that she doesn't want me in there with her. But damn I just want to wrap my arms around her, lift her into my chest, and kiss her.

"Hey," I hear the whisper coming from the end of the hallway as a slight light fades from one of the rooms. It's too dark to see who exactly it is but I already know it's Ollie. I prop myself on my elbows as she leans farther into the hallway waving, indicating for me to follow.

"Can't sleep?" she asks as I get closer to her, and I shake my head no, wanting to remain silent so as not to wake anyone else up. Once we close the door to her bedroom, she gestures to the big bed in the middle of the room. This room is such an adult room and so different from the setup of the childhood rooms she and her brothers had back in Fisher Creek.

Her bedroom is full of very light neutral earthy tones, paired with a beautiful tree in the corner next to her desk by the window. She climbs onto the bed and gently pats the made side for me to sit next to her. I slowly walk around the bed taking in her sheer beauty. I'm always amazed at how makeup for many has become a necessity whether they use it as a way to impress someone else or feel good about themselves. Ollie has never been like that. She grew up on the farm and while Penelope was always using makeup and taking ages to get ready, Ollie never saw the point in it since she's going to either sweat it off or get dirty anyway.

Looking at her now in her little black silk pajama set as she sits crisscross on her bed and pulls up the blanket over her lap, I can't get into the bed fast enough.

"Me either." She shrugs. "I couldn't get my brain to turn off the idea of kissing you."

I feel the ache in my chest at that line, because, well, same. Instead of replying with words, I lean over, turn her face toward me, and kiss her. The kiss is full of passion, and lust and instantly brings me back to that night doing karaoke in Fisher Creek.

She melts into my arms, bringing one hand up to the side of my face, the other hand pressed firmly against my chest. My hands reach to pull her onto my lap. Her silk pajamas don't leave much to the imagination as the thin black material hangs loosely over her hardening nipples. She straddles my lap rubbing against my already erect dick through my gym shorts. Leaning up against her headboard is perfect to allow both my hands to wander across her perfect body, reaching up and giving a gentle pinch to her nipple. She lets out the faintest little gasp separating our lips and giving me a devious smile.

"This okay?" I ask quietly.

"Mm-hmm," she slides off my lap and down toward the end of the bed, moving my shorts and boxers down in one swift motion.

Chapter 30

OLIVIA

"Shit, shit, shit!" I whisper loudly as I wake up around eight in the morning with Noah's giant leg across mine. My head is nestled against his chest and his arm around my shoulder. I knew he was in my bed but I meant to kick him back to the couch before anyone else got up. I'm not ashamed of Noah, or the night we shared, but I still don't understand my feelings and I don't want to explain that to anyone else yet.

"Noah, wake up!" I say, wiggling out from under him.

"Huh? Ollie, what is going on?" Noah asks groggily, wiping his eyes.

"We fell asleep, and unless you want to explain to Cole..." I start, but Noah just tips his head back toward the ceiling and laughs as if this is a laughing matter.

I'm stunned silent by his reaction and just sit there staring at him.

When he doesn't stop laughing I eventually ask "Why is this funny to you?" with more than a morsel of annoyance

"Ollie, I think everyone in this house expected me to end up in this bed last night, and Cole is the last person who is going to question that" he replies, smiling at me. His answer only confuses me more because Cole has only ever shown distaste for any form of PDA or affection we show each other.

"What do you mean?" I reply.

"Ollie, he knows everything." His face dropped into a very serious look I haven't seen in years. Since that night in Oklahoma. Nope. Not getting into that right now. When I don't answer him right away, he continues "He didn't tell you?"

I shake my head in response, not sure exactly where this is going.

He sighs and mumbles something about Cole being an asshole, a loyal asshole but an asshole, nonetheless.

I jump out of bed and stand near the wall at the side of the bed. Noah sees my confusion and concern on my face and gets up. After walking over to me, he takes my hand and leads me to the door of the bedroom.

"Come on, let's go wake him up," Noah says as he leads me to the living room where we find Cole sitting upright with a cup of coffee on the couch, Caroline's on the counter barstool with her tea, and both are smirking at us like they just won the jackpot.

"Based on the terrified look, Ollie, I'd wager she's hoping to sneak you back out here before anyone is awake," Cole says to Noah.

"Well, I figured you told her that you knew. You talk at least once a week and are attached at the hip," he fires back with a hint of irritation in his tone.

I don't think I've ever seen the two of them argue or talk to each other in any sort of tone.

"Not my story to tell," Cole replies with a shrug.

"Okay, okay, okay. Enough, you two. You are worse than brothers. Jesus," Caroline jumps in, trying to keep the peace but also making sure I don't lose my shit. She knows I don't handle confrontation well and when it comes to these two, I absolutely cannot handle it. Both men stop, Noah drops my arm and turns to look at Caroline with a scowl.

"Since this conversation has started, you're both going to tell Olivia whatever secret you're keeping, and I'm going to stay here to moderate and make sure she's not getting hurt here," Caroline says with a stern voice. She's one of those friends who you consider the "mean friend." The ones you want by your side, especially in situations like this because we both know she'll bury a body for me if it keeps me safe and happy.

Noah and Cole glance at each other and then we all venture onto the sectional. Caroline hands me a coffee, as we sit on the left side of the sectional under a throw blanket. The boys sit on the opposite side of the couch looking at each other unsure of where to start.

"I guess we just start from the beginning. Cole, tell Ollie where you found me the week after she came back to the city," Noah says, unable to look at me, but sharing a pointed look with Caroline. It's a stare that screams he's sorry and that he would never hurt me.

Caroline, however, doesn't forgive and forget easily. She was there for the trauma from ten years ago and understands that this could entirely ruin me.

There is an overwhelming sense of anxiety and terror that devours me as we sit here in anticipation of what Cole has to say. Did Cole find Noah's tongue deep in another woman? Why does that make me want to crumble? Assuming is not going to get me anywhere so I need to focus on the moment and listen.

"At the firehouse, running on the treadmill, ten sheets to the wind," Cole answers finally, after Noah gives him a nod.

Noah's head hangs in embarrassment and shame from his actions. And before they even get the chance to explain, I blurt out.

"What were you thinking? Noah, that is incredibly unsafe. You could've been seriously injured, and then what would you have done? You'd be out of work, unable to fix your house. What on earth were you thinking?"

Caroline places her hand on my forearm with a sincere look of empathy on her face. I can't tell if it's toward me or knowing the rest of this story. I realize that any hope of hiding my feelings and whatever this is between us has gone completely out the window.

"That's exactly what Cole said before he made me get off the treadmill, gave me a verbal warning and a write up. He then sat me down to chat with him. He was worried I would be a risk to not only myself but everyone in the department and he wasn't wrong, I don't know if I had been sober a single moment since you left at this point," Noah begins to say. "And I realized at that moment, I was hitting rock bottom again. If anyone was going to help me get back on track and give me any shot at showing you I love you and I'm not going anywhere, it would be Cole. So I told him everything. Every moment from the night in Oklahoma, to Jarred and the letter, to our times over Christmas. Everything. But most importantly, I'm undeniably, deeply in love with you Ollie. I always have been and I will never stop loving you," he finishes, all in one breath before anyone can interject.

My jaw hits the floor, Caroline's grip tightens on my arm and Cole is looking at Noah with a proud look on his face because he knows how hard this has been for Noah.

"That cannot be true, in Oklahoma..." I start to say. He didn't love me then, he couldn't have possibly loved me for ten years after.

"I know, Ollie. I know what I said in Oklahoma. And I promise you I've regretted it every day since then," he says.

"What did you say in Oklahoma?" Caroline asks.

Realizing I never told them the entirety of what happened ten years ago. It's not until this moment when I'm seeing red that I thought I could never tell someone everything that happened that weekend.

"He told me he didn't love me and that we could never actually be together." I hiss out, full of wrath and anger, remembering back to that day. Caroline's face reddens and she squeezes my arm in solidarity as I glare across the room to Noah.

He looks down, and Cole speaks up before Noah has the chance to say anything.

"Liv, did you ever let me know to explain that day to you? Or have you just been holding a grudge deeming him the worst for the last ten years?" There's a certain bite to his words that tells me I've hit a nerve with him, and that maybe I don't know everything that happened. But that doesn't change the fact that I was heartbroken after Oklahoma or it took me months to really get back to myself again.

"You're right, Olivia, that is exactly what I said. You had just started college at Marquette, I was graduating basic training and had no idea where I was about to be stationed. That first night you were there, I was so excited to see you. Finally hold you in my arms again after those ten agonizing weeks away from you. You spent the whole time telling me about these amazing people you met at school, and how all of your classes were going but also how you were going to finish out the semester and then transition to online classes until we were settled in a place long enough for you to go back to school." Caroline lifts her hand off my arm, having never known that was my plan. I feel my eyes fill with tears but I can't tear my eyes from Noah's face as he continues speaking. "You were going to put your entire career and life on hold for me. To be the wife of someone in the military who may not even be in the same country as you. Who may not even come home? Ollie, I couldn't let you do that and I knew you would never change your mind, once you get your heart set on something it's impossible to change it. So I did the only thing I could think of and that was to make you hate me. You wouldn't give up everything if you hated me. Did I have to give up the one person who meant the most to me in return? Yes, and I would do it again. Ollie, I have loved you since the moment we met in the cafeteria that one day. I'm sorry for the hurt I've caused you. I will regret that until the day I die. But I loved you then. I love you now. And I will never stop loving you, Olivia Bennett," he finishes with silent tears running down his face, and it suddenly hits me that, *holy shit*, this man broke his own heart for me.

Caroline continues to ask questions and interrogate Cole and Noah but the sound of their voices sounds like they are talking underwater as I'm entirely engulfed by one sentence.

He loves me and he never stopped loving me.

"Liv, you okay?" I hear Cole ask as he walks over from the couch.

Nodding my head yes, bringing myself back to reality, I sink into the couch and try to decipher my emotions. Am I sad? Yes. Am I angry? Hell yes. Am I grateful he finally told me the truth? Absolutely.

"That wasn't your decision to make." I bite tears back from my eyes, damning them with all of my heart. I do not want to cry right now.

"I know, Ollie. And I am truly sorry for taking that choice away from you. There was never a letter, phone call, text message, or even a single day where I didn't think of you. When things were bad, and people died, thinking about you was the only light back into my life. I know I hurt you. I know what I did was stupid and it wasn't fair to you that I hid the truth from you for all these years, but I was stupid and afraid. I thought it would be better if you never thought about me again instead of worrying about if I was alive or giving up your entire life for someone who might not even make it to tomorrow."

I can't stop the tears from streaming down my face now and I move from my side of the couch to his, where he still silently cries as he confesses everything. I sit next to him placing my hands on his forearm and take a second to get my thoughts together.

Cole and Caroline relocate down the hall to give us privacy but I know they're standing at the end of the hallway to eavesdrop.

"Noah, I am angry that you took that decision away from me, that you robbed us from ten years of what could have been an amazing time together. But I'm also adult enough to know that we wouldn't have worked back then if we stayed together. That I needed to grow up and become who I am today before committing to my forever love story." Tears continue to stream down his cheeks and he doesn't as much as breathe a word. "I know that in those three days over Christmas I was the happiest I've been in ten years and I'm not just saying that because you are the best sex I've ever had. You make me smile, make me feel seen in ways no one has ever done before, and continue to love me through it all. I will forever be grateful that my annoying brother spilled the beans about my coming home," I continue.

"Yes!" I hear Cole whisper loudly from the hallway with presumably a matching enthusiastic fist bump. Noah chuckles in response as I roll my eyes, and I know our time is going to be limited moving forward.

"Because I have never stopped thinking about you. I have never stopped loving you, Noah. And yes, I'm afraid. I am afraid it won't work out. I'm afraid I wont be able to trust that you won't hurt me again, but I also know that I'm willing to try," I finally finish, and before I can move, Noah pulls me into his lap, fully engulfing me in a hug.

Chapter 31

NOAH

After finally telling the truth to Ollie, admitting I'll always love her, and owning up to my previous actions, the idea of leaving her in Milwaukee sounds atrocious. The excitement around finally having the opportunity to properly date the girl of my dreams, my sister's best friend, and her giving me a second chance is enough for me to sell my house, quit my job, and stay in the city forever. I feel a huge weight off my shoulders and am ecstatic to continue this adventure with Ollie while we figure our relationship out.

The drive back to Fisher Creek is only two hours but Cole insists on driving even though he's done nothing but complain about having to sleep on the couch and having a sore back as a result. The amount he's talking makes me suspicious that something happened after I went to Ollie's room.

We're listening to his old rock playlist and he is popping back and forth in his seat while drumming on the steering wheel. He's such a dork.

I snort at him as he continues to jam my mind shifting back to Ollie and her car dance moves. She used to steal the aux cord in my car playing whatever artist she was obsessed with that week, singing at the top of her lungs. I should add that she's a terrible singer but she didn't care. Her carefree energy when we were in the car was something that I loved the most about her. She would move her hand like a wave to the beat of the song but also the way the car was moving. Thinking back to Ollie and the way things used to be causing my face to heat and a smile creep onto my face.

"What the hell is wrong with your face?" Cole asks, looking at me with a cocky smile on it.

"Shut up," I reply. Not wanting to tell him I was thinking about Ollie but not knowing how to change the subject I say, "Also, did you know Caroline was that terrifying?" I laugh trying to lighten the mood.

He does nothing but laugh in response, a nervous laugh that confirms my suspicions. Cole's never been able to keep a secret. If his life depended on him to keep his mouth shut, he'd have died thousands of times now. Thankfully he isn't a cat with only nine lives.

"Did you and Caroline...?" I ask directly. There's no point in trying to beat around the bush because I know he's going to crack before we get back to Fisher Creek. Plus, I've always been blunt, probably to a fault but it's better to just know than beat around the bush.

Cole's face turns red and I know I hit the nail on the head. He doesn't answer and I decide it's probably better I don't need to know what happens between them. They don't want to tell anyone yet and I certainly cannot keep this from Ollie.

But there's also a part of me that is curious, because as far as I'm aware Cole hasn't dated anyone since Layla, and that ended at least seven years ago.

"I don't think I've seen you like this about a girl since Layla," I say, wanting to get an update on the situation.

Layla Chaney's family owns the golf course on the far side of the lake, and the Bennett family sold cranberries to them for their club-house. Cole and Layla met in middle school, and I swear they were going to be together until they weren't.

Cole's face falls into a scowl and he changes his percussion from matching the beat of the song to a nervous tap before looking at me and saying, "She reached out this morning.

"For what?" I almost yell, in response. I may not have been in town or even on speaking terms with Cole when everything went to shit but I heard enough to know that if Layla even considers walking back into his life, we'd all have a problem with it.

"She lives in the city and saw that we were at the bar last night in my stories. Said she wanted to check in and see how things were going." The look on his face tells me he is extremely unsure of what to think about this entire situation. Cole was convinced he and Layla were going to be married, even had a ring ready to propose when she finished college. So when she abruptly ended their relationship, he was heartbroken. I know he'll always have a place in his heart for Layla and the growing up they did together, but she needs to drop off the face of the earth.

"I didn't realize you still talked," I respond, trying to be encouraging and also friendly.

"We don't," he whispers as if unsure if it's a real fact or just a dream.

"We haven't spoken since she told me off for asking questions about her reason for breaking up. That was basically seven full years ago. I honestly didn't even know she still follows me."

I make a mental note to continue checking in with him and to keep plugging Caroline because while she is a terrifying person, she at least loves with her heart.

Hearing his stomach growl, I realize we didn't eat breakfast, or anything for that matter this morning and reach into my backpack to find a snack. Feeling grateful for Ollie's constant need to care for those around her and her little snack bag she packed us as if we were going to be driving across the state.

His stomach growls again, this time louder, as if it knows I'm looking for a snack. Cole clasps his hand over his stomach, trying to quiet it as I open the brown paper bag, finding not only a large supply of granola bars and sour gummy candy but also a small folded up piece of paper.

"Here, eat this before you turn into a monster," I say, handing him a chocolate chip peanut butter granola bar. My heart starts to beat faster as I look at the folded up piece of paper unsure of what to expect. Part of me is terrified she's changed her mind and wants to protect her heart while the other part of me is excited knowing it's not.

My fingers fumble the paper as I attempt to unfold it, and I feel Cole's side eye and judgement as he silently laughs at my new found clumsiness.

Hi :) I thought since letters kept us whole ten years ago, it would be fun to bring them back now. And idk about you but I still have all those letters from boot camp, which might be embarrassing...but whatever. I just wanted to say thanks for coming up with Cole this weekend and telling me the truth. <3 Ollie

I cannot help but smile knowing she kept the letters. Mine stay in the same keepsake box as Jarred's tags and letter and I'd always reread them when feeling beaten down and broken from the military. Ollie's been the only consistent factor keeping me sane through the years.

Chapter 32

OLIVIA

It's easy to fall back into my routine of running, work, reading, sleep, and repeat. Each day feels lighter knowing Noah was truly in this for the long hall. I may not fully trust him yet, or be prepared to jump head-first into this relationship quite yet but the thought of a future makes me happy.

Work's been smooth, the new patients actively participate in their care, and are excited to do it at home. All of us in the office have been getting lunch together and we're planning a huge community outreach event to do in a few weeks, to support an underprivileged area. This is uncommon because, typically, my entire office sticks to themselves, does their job, and goes home for the day. I love my job and my place of employment but it would be nice to have more camaraderie amongst us. Create a family within the office, because it's true that I spend more time with these people than my own family or friends.

I'm just coming back into the office after lunch with Mason and Savannah on a Thursday when my phone starts to ring. I pull it out of my scrub top pocket and see that it's Cole. I normally would think that him calling me in the middle of a work day was weird but we just found out Penelope is getting divorced and she and the boys are moving home, so we've been chatting almost every day.

"Hey!" I say as I answer the phone.

There is a brief moment of silence before I hear him say "Liv" in a super low tone. Before he has the opportunity to say anything else I've put him on speaker and start sprinting to my car as I text the office manager.

Something is wrong.

"What's wrong, Cole?" I snap a little out of breath from the sprint.

"We had a call today, the old shed down Jameson Road caught fire," he starts to tell me, and I feel every ounce of my heart sink.

Someone died. I know every member of that fire department. I know no matter who it is, I have to get home. We are family.

"Who?" I ask, yelling at this point.

Silence.

Then I hear a gulp as his voice shakes a little.

"Noah, Liv. It's Noah."

I can't speak, I feel like I can't breathe, like there are walls closing in on me.

"He's okay, his leg is injured, and he definitely had some smoke inhalation but he is okay. We're at the hospital with Mom right now to make sure."

The panic is filling my body from head to toe, I'm shaking and probably shouldn't be driving my car at this point but I'm on autopilot tearing through the parking lot on my way home to see for myself.

After an hour of driving, most of which was probably considered reckless, I pull into the hospital parking lot, when it all hits me. I haven't been in this hospital since Grandma died. Since my entire world shattered and I can feel it shattering all over again. The wave of emotions crashing over me.

The overwhelming feeling of helplessness as she lay in this hospital, her body finally failing her years after her mind did. The fear in knowing she was suffering, hating the state she's in but also not ready to let her go. Let her leave our family, let her leave me. The helplessness quickly turned into anger for all the same reasons I was heartbroken.

I feel my body freeze as I get out of my car, the same time I see Cole outside pacing back and forth. The moment he sees me he jogs over, engulfing me in a hug.

"Me too," he whispers as I start to fight back tears. I wonder if this will ever get any easier. Will it ever be possible to set foot in this hospital without drowning in emotion and heartbreak?

Cole pulls away from our hug, emotions written all over his face which quickly turns into a soft smile and a laugh as he says,

"He is going to be pissed that I called you".

"He can be as pissed as he wants. I would be here regardless," I huff with a roll of my eyes. Noah has always made a stink when people fuss over him and will do everything in his power to avoid it.

Cole turns me toward the door, wrapping his arm around my shoulder like the amazing supportive big brother he is and looks at me and says, "Let's tackle this beast."

Then we walk toward the hospital door. I have no idea if he is referring to the hospital as a whole or Noah. But either way, I can't help but chuckle to myself as we make our way in.

Mom meets us halfway down the hallway to where the people who are admitted are. I'm confused as to why he was admitted if it "wasn't bad."

I start to tense up when Mom says, "Relax, it's precautionary for the smoke inhalation. They took him to get x-rays and we're scheduling an MRI."

My mother has worked at his hospital for as long as I can remember and is an absolutely amazing nurse. She can read the room and meet not only the patients but their families where they are to give support, but she can also give critical information without bullshitting anything. I feel my heart rate continue to race in my chest, knowing it isn't going to calm down until I see him for myself.

"He's being a bear of a human so just be ready for that, Liv," she finishes.

I've seen Noah in one of his absolute worst moments and there's no doubt in my mind that I can handle whatever he decides to throw at us today.

"Come one, let's go wait in his room until he gets back," Mom says putting her arm on my back.

Before we even get to the threshold into the room, I hear, "No. Go home, Ollie," coming from behind me as we approach the door to his room.

Cole looks at me and whispers "He's already kicked out every other member of the fire department."

We step to the side of the hallway allowing the nurse to push him in his wheelchair back to the room. I give her an apologetic look, knowing full well that he has been bitching about the wheelchair since they made him use it in the first place. The poor girl just gives us a cautionary look in response.

"Thanks, Alissa," Mom says when we all get back into the hospital room. "I can take him from here for now."

Alissa nods politely and quickly turns to leave the room, confirming what we all knew, Noah is being a royal pain in the ass about everything.

He doesn't even look at me before grumbling at Cole, "Why the fuck did you call her? I told you not to."

Cole looks ashamed, defeated, and torn between his best friend and his sister and there is no way I'm letting Noah get away with hurting him. Not today.

"Hold on. You get to be grumpy because you're hurt and you are in pain but you do not get to yell at anyone in the room or this hospital anymore today. They're here to help you, and by the looks of that leg, you need all the help you can get right now. So let's retry that statement again," I interject before this conversation gets any more out of hand.

Mom and Cole look at each other, eyes big, shocked by my interjection. I have always been the shy, quiet girl afraid of confrontation so to see me stand up big and tall to the boy, well, man now who I have followed around forever is shocking.

Instead of responding, he scowls and stares at me, waiting for me to crack but what he doesn't know is this is my everyday life and I will not break. Mom gently elbows Cole to prompt him to leave the room and give us some privacy.

"Good luck," Cole murmurs as he passes by mem and Mom squeezes my forearm in reassurance before leaving.

Back to the silence. Back to the grumpy scowl and stare. It takes everything in me not to walk over to him and do a once-over myself before we continue this conversation. I can't help but gaze over his entire body to do a brief check and when I get to his face, I notice he is now looking at the floor. He's no longer scowling or looking like the big angry bear he had been moments before. He looks embarrassed and ashamed.

It breaks my heart to see him like this. I walk over to where he is sitting in his chair and kneel next to him trying to look at his face.

"Ollie," he says sternly, avoiding eye contact.

I soften my voice and place my hand on his knee. "Yes?"

"Why are you here?"

"Because Cole called me."

"Cole calls you every day."

"Yes?"

"So why did you come running in the middle of the day?"

"Because I care about you, and you literally could have died today, Noah."

"I didn't."

I want to smack him for his smart-ass comment not knowing if he is joking or genuinely still trying to convince me to leave.

"So, go home, Ollie," he says before I have the chance to respond.

"I'm not going anywhere. You can be mad at me and hate me tomorrow or the next day but right now you need someone to keep you from ripping that nurse's head off," I say. "And especially not until I know for a fact that you're okay."

"I'm fine," Noah replies with a raspy cough.

"Clearly," I say, rolling my eyes. "Why don't you tell me what's going on? Why do you want me to leave?"

He still refuses to look at me and lets out a deep sigh. My patience is starting to thin because ultimately we are adults and this is childish. I understand he's in pain and maybe embarrassed that the injury happened in the first place, but come on, let's use our big boy words and say what we mean.

"Noah."

He sighs again, sensing my annoyance when I stand up and move away from him. "It was my first real call with the department, and I messed up and got trapped. They got me out, which is great, but not at the risk of other members of the team. Cole is the one who moved the beam so I could get out. Ollie, would you still be standing there if I made it out and he didn't because he was saving me?" he attacks, pain lacing his voice. It comes deep from within his heart and I know this is about significantly more than just being injured and me showing up.

Jarred.

"Cole isn't Jarred. Noah, you are alive, Cole is alive. I know you're reliving what is one of the worst days of your life, but you also know you cannot live in the past. It's the past for a reason. Jarred wouldn't want that, Cole doesn't want that. Whatever happened to talking about your feelings and emotions? Because you can't control how you feel but you can control how you react to them." I say as carefully as possible, not wanting to send him into a downward spiral, but still hoping he'll remember when he said it to me.

I can see his wheels turning and I know he's remembering that day and I can't help but wonder if the Army hardened that side of him. Does Dr. Doyle work with more than just military loss? Do they consider all aspects of a military personnel's life, past, present, and future?

"We weren't advised to share and talk a lot about our feelings and it has been something Dr. Doyle and I have been working on over the last six months."

Mom and Cole knock on the door as they round the corner with Dr. Armington, the local orthopedic surgeon. Dr. Armington is the surgeon who did my knee surgery in high school and I have a slight panic that this is the route we're about to go with Noah.

"Olivia, hi, what a nice surprise!"

"Hi Dr. Armington, I hope you are well. Do you have an update on Noah's knee?" I ask probably too quickly because I have zero patience and need to know what we're dealing with.

Mom looks at me with a disappointed look, as if I'm being rude, but frankly, I don't care. I need to know so we can get Noah the help he needs without risking a downward spiral. I work with EMS and first responders daily and it's critical to get all of the answers upfront so they can prepare to be out of work, and for when they're going to come back.

"Good news! There is a mild sprain of the ACL and MCL, but surgery is not required. I recommend staying off that knee for the next two weeks entirely and starting a physical therapy program as quickly as possible. But you are looking at four to six weeks of recovery," Dr. Armington says.

There isn't a physical therapy clinic in Fisher Creek, and I know finding somewhere to go plus transportation has been almost impossible in the past. I place a hand on Noah's shoulder, thank Dr. Armington, and hope they get the hint to leave.

"Why don't we call Dr. Doyle and see if he has any emergency availability this week to check in with you? Then I will get you home and we'll start getting everything set up for the next two weeks," I say to Noah, already starting to pack everything up and look up Dr. Doyle's number.

Noah doesn't move, doesn't look up, doesn't speak in response, and I know this is where I have to be right now.

Chapter 33

NOAH

What the actual fuck was Cole thinking calling Ollie today?

She has a career, friends, and her own life to worry about, the last thing she needs is to fuss over me.

Especially when I'm fine.

A little swelling and bruising is nothing. I had worse in basic training let alone in active duty. Hell, their mom is even here. Granted, she works at this hospital and was in fact working today but still, they're all being a little ridiculous.

The only problem is it's hard to be mad at the girl you love when she comes running because she's worried about you, even if she says she doesn't trust you enough to be dating yet. It's even worse when she stands up to you for being a dick to the people trying to help you.

God damn, she was hot when she did that.

If I could've stood in that moment, I would have pulled her close, clutched that perfect ass in both hands and planted a kiss on her lips. Thank god I'm stuck in this chair and no one can see my arousal.

But that's beside the point, I don't want Ollie to see me like this. It's one thing for her to be here when I have an injury, but to be here when I'm injured, unable to walk, and spiraling back down into that same dark place I was in after Jarred. I didn't want her to see me then, and I certainly don't want her to see me now circling that drain.

I really need to call Doyle this week to keep me from my dark cave. Today was just too similar to Jarred. I get it Cole is fine, he is alive, but Jarred is only dead because he was trying to save all of our asses…costing him his own. The rest of our squad was able to escape the carnage of the bomb because he stayed and that's the only image I could see today when Cole was lifting the beam off my leg except this time it was Cole. The brother of the girl I'm trying to win back and killing her brother definitely would not win me any points.

I feel weak and angry. Weak that I cannot control these emotions and that I'm having them in the first place. Weak that I wasn't able to move the beam and get out myself. And angry. Angry at the fact I have these feelings, that Jarred's accident has such a huge toll on my life still. Angry that Cole risked himself for me. Angry that he called Ollie. And even angrier that everything she said is true.

Even today, ten years later, she can still read me like a book and knows me the best.

Except then, that damn Dr. Armington came in and told me that I'm going to be out for the next four to six weeks and the ice broke. It feels like I fell through the ice on the lake and am now stuck under the frigid water unable to breathe. Unable to move, to break free from this overwhelming and all-consuming feeling of helplessness. What am I going to do for the next four to six weeks if I can't work? I'm really going to spiral.

What does Ollie mean by, *"I will get you home and we start getting everything set up for the next two weeks"*? Like hell, I'm going to let her stay here for two weeks. I have always been the caretaker in my family, especially after my dad passed. I got Bec to and from school, to and from dance, made lunches, even got Mom out of bed on the hardest of days. Never once was someone there to take care of me, and I absolutely despise the feeling of Ollie doing that for me.

Ollie and Mrs. Bennett go with Dr. Armington to complete my discharge papers and get any post-smoke inhalation care instructions I may need. Which basically entails sucking on cough drops, resting, and avoiding any type of smoke. All of these are basically a given considering I live alone, don't smoke, and am on crutches so it's not like I can do anything fun that I want to do.

They fit me for a big bulky brace to wear for the first few weeks to maintain stability as I go through rehab, and for the awful crutches I think are probably a bigger risk than me just walking in the first place, but I let them remember Ollie yelling at me earlier.

"Hey, at least it's not surgery," Cole says as I hobble out into the hall to find everyone else. I know he's trying to lighten the mood and assure me that everything is okay but I really just want to punch him. Thankfully, I'm spending all my energy concentrating on not falling with these stupid crutches.

"Yeah," I manage to grunt out in response.

"I'm sorry that I called her, Noah. But you need her here for this."

I know he's right but I'm not going to admit that.

I ride home with Ollie, Cole following close behind in his car, and Ms. Bennett remained at the hospital to catch up on some work after spending hours with me.

"Yes, Mother, I'm fine. Ollie and Cole are getting me back to the house and set up for rest and PT," I say into my phone, almost annoyed. My mother means well and we have always been close, but since I joined the Army and now the fire department and Bec spending her winters at the ski resort helping with rescues and teaching people how to navigate the more difficult, tree-filled routes, she's become a little overbearing. I get it, losing the love of her life absolutely broke her and I can't imagine how she would feel if something happened to either of her children but it can be a lot.

Ollie chuckles from the driver's seat, sensing my annoyance, but also gives me a disapproving look that screams, *Noah, be nice to your mother she only cares about you.*

"Yeah, Ollie is here. No, you cannot call her, Mom. I'm fine. Okay, Mom, we are pulling down the driveway, I'm going to hang up now. I will see you soon. Bye, Mom." I hang up the before she even has the opportunity to respond.

"We are not pulling down your driveway," Ollie says, glancing over to me.

I'm trying to get comfortable in the front of her tiny little sedan with this god-awful brace while keeping my leg mostly straight. I had to slide the seat as far back as it would go to fit here. They tried to get me to sit in the backseat so I could comfortably sit sideways, but I was not about to get chauffeured back to Fisher Creek. I may be injured but I'm not helpless.

Chapter 34

OLIVIA

"**I** don't know, guys. There is such a huge need for physical therapy in the rural areas. I always had access to it when growing up because Mom works at the hospital but otherwise, almost no one in Fisher Creek or its surrounding towns have access to it," I say before sipping my peppermint and lemon tea.

I spent a week at home with Noah and ultimately Cole, who I swear is worse than any helicopter parent out there getting him acclimated to his crutches at home and learning the first set of the rehabilitation program we are using. I'm facilitating his physical therapy on the grounds that he actually does it, which is where Cole comes in. The main thing I need him to do is to rest, relax, and not overdo it even if it means he goes a little stir-crazy.

He had one appointment with Dr. Doyle while I was there and was scheduled for another this week to continue growth within his mental health and stability. I'm incredibly proud of him and every step he is taking to better himself.

"You're not wrong, but what are you going to do about it?" Caroline says, cutting a piece of her chocolate muffin. We're sitting at our favorite coffee shop, having breakfast, and chatting about everything that has happened over the last week. Caroline thinks I have absolutely lost my marbles for running to help the day Cole called, saying it made me seem desperate and obsessed. And for someone who claims she hates this man and everything that has happened between us that is not the action I would be doing.

I just roll my eyes every time she mentions this because I know she is right and again I refuse to admit that or get involved with that conversation.

"She's right, Liv. It's not like you're going to drop everything and open your own practice in Fisher Creek," Savannah chimes in with a slight chuckle. She's obviously joking but what they didn't know is that is exactly what I want to do.

"Oh my god. She is," Caroline screeches when I don't say anything. They both drop their utensils and stare at me.

"It's not set in stone, but yeah, I'm thinking about it. No one knows about it besides my family and I want to keep it that way in case it doesn't work out. But we went and looked at a building downtown right before I left and honestly, it would be absolutely perfect for my dream office."

They just continue to stare at me, entirely stunned. I can't tell if they're mad, shocked, excited, confused, or all of the above.

"You really have thought this out, haven't you?" Caroline asks.

"Yeah, it won't be open for a while, there's a lot of work that needs to be done. It just also means that I'll be traveling back and forth to Fisher Creek more."

They look at each other and smiles begin to form on their faces. This feels like a drastic change from their initial reaction.

"To spend more time with Noah?" they ask simultaneously. Caroline got it out of me about spending the night together when he and Cole were in Milwaukee, and now they feel the unnecessary need to bring it up any chance they can.

"I will be focusing more on getting the office ready to open, but his being there will be an added plus." I learned very quickly I may as well play into their obsession with my not-relationship-relationship instead of arguing about us not actually being together.

"Olivia, we're actually so happy for you. You've always wanted to own an office yourself, and you need to get out of your current environment, it doesn't feed you. Plus, seeing you with Noah the other day confirms he is your home, and your happiness, and there is no denying the connection you two have," Savannah says as she grabs my hand on the table. She's always been a sweet, shy, supportive friend.

"We will absolutely miss you so much, but the house is getting a little crowded anyway," Caroline says with some fierceness, but also full of love.

"Guys, I'm not moving to Mars," I say in retort. "I'll only be two hours away and nothing is official yet. I have always dreamed about making a difference in people's lives and I always thought that the biggest difference I could make was in a big city working with officials and important people. What I have learned in the last week is that I can make the biggest change in the lives and my community in my hometown. Feeding into the people and community that fed into me."

My phone dings and it's the daily Noah photo the boys send me to prove he is doing his exercises. I didn't ask them to do this, but if it keeps them consistent and laughing then I absolutely condone it. Today, it looks like at the firehouse gym, Noah is sitting on the floor, wearing nothing but olive green sweatpants that fit a little too perfectly doing his knee presses. He has a scowl on his face but it isn't a *grumpy,*

I hate this scowl, it's more of a *concentrated and focused* scowl as he tries to retrain that brain-body connection.

I feel my body start to heat and a tingle creep up from inside as I look at the photo of Noah, because it's a selfie completely ruined by Cole's goofy-looking smile in the bottom left corner where he's pointing to Noah on the floor behind him.

Before they're given the opportunity to call me out for blushing this hard, I turn my phone to Caroline and Savannah.

"Look at that ridiculous face," Caroline comments. I can't help but wonder if anything has ever happened between them over the years, they always find some way to be next to each other when we go out and are always up before everyone else. That part doesn't surprise me because if I thought I was an early riser, Caroline likes to get up in the middle of the night to start her day.

I put my phone down and think about how grateful I'm to have these friends, who've been there to embrace me at my worst, support me through the regrowth and finding myself again, and push me to follow those dreams every day.

Chapter 35

OLIVIA

Noah's been doing really well with his therapy. Doing each exercise consistently, compliantly, and even asking for modifications when necessary. Cole's gone every day to check in and see how things are going, helping with minor details like shoveling snow, and even bringing Noah to the station a few times to run through his approved routine at the gym there.

If there is one thing I have learned through treating competitive athletes and professionals, it's that you never tell them they can't do any form of activity. They will go stir crazy, they won't actually listen to you and they will end up hurt more than they started. This is why I also have Noah go through some low-weight upper-body exercises to help maintain his fitness level throughout his recovery.

We talked almost every day some days more extensively than others, and more than just about his knee and injury. It feels like we're starting to get back to our old friendship again. Making plans to do our favorite activities in Milwaukee and Fisher Creek.

I'm impressed with the progress he's made in the last few weeks and I'm super excited to hear that Dr. Armington has cleared him to start walking full weight again so that we can actually do one of the plans off our list. We made a shared note on our phones so we can each add to it when we think of an idea. Noah changed the name of the note from *Activities* to *Dates* and I couldn't help but roll my eyes initially, but there's also a part deep inside me that warmed from the core, as if the blood in my body was molten lava heating me from the inside out.

Dates:

1. Milwaukee Art Museum

2. Walk around Fisher Lake - snowball fight optional

3. Painting my kitchen

I laugh as I pull up the list to determine what activity we should do first, seeing *painting my kitchen* as a new addition on the list, knowing exactly where his brain was going when he added it. Can't say I'd be opposed to another painting day, it's been ages since our last night together, even longer since the painting day, and I feel like I'm growing cobwebs.

"What are you laughing at?" Caroline asks from the other side of the island.

My face reddens as I hand her my phone showing her the list.

"Subtle, ha-ha." She laughs in response. Caroline may have torn Noah's head off last time they were together but she is the biggest Noah fan there is. Wanting my happiness, she is constantly pushing me to trust him a little more and give us an opportunity. I just don't know if I can ever fully trust him the way I used to.

"He got cleared to start walking full weight and drive again. So we have to pick something to do. We are determining which is better, Milwaukee or Fisher Creek and let's be honest, we all know the city is the place to be," I respond. "Help me come up with more activities to prove that to him."

"There is nothing to prove, since he is wrong." she says as she begins walking back down the hallway to her room.

4. Book Binding Class

5. Paint and Sip

6. Tasting at Bobbers

7. Mitchell Park Domes

8. Kneland-Bennett Family BBQ

I freeze as I read the rest of the list. It's already almost April, and we are definitely going to still have snow on the ground but it also means that the annual barbeque is in less than two months. Our families have maintained their friendship over the years even when Noah and I did not. The family barbeque is always at the end of May or beginning of June to simulate the start of the change of weather into summer. Noah and I haven't attended the event since the one during my senior year of high school. I always made excuses not to attend, whether it be being busy with school or work, or having a migraine, but in truth I never went because of the possibility that Noah would be there. Penelope and Cole made sure to do their recon to let me know well in advance if he would be home.

Now, we're both home and we are on good terms. We can both go to the party this year. However, part of me is afraid to be thrown back into that environment, will it be weird spending time with Ms. Kneland? I know I saw her briefly over the holidays but to actually spend consistent time with her? Will they accept me back into their life like I was in high school? The other part of me, the bigger part feels relieved. Relieved that I don't have to hide from my family, from the people who meant the most to me. I'll be able to bring Mason,

Caroline, and Savannah, and not have to come up with an excuse as to why we couldn't go other than the fact that Noah is home.

That is when it finally hits me, avoiding someone important to you, to live in the past is absolutely exhausting.

I take out my phone and text Noah.

> **Me: What should our first activity be?**

He wastes no time replying

> **Noah: Activity? Do you mean date?**

> **Me: Yes. What activity do you want to do?**

I hope he feels the emphasis I tried to place on the activity.

> **Noah: You.**

I smirk, even though I have no idea how to respond to that. But we really do need to make a plan for the weekend and we really shouldn't be intimate. If therapy has taught me anything over the last decade it's that we need to commit to the emotional side of a relationship and determine if the connection is actually there aside from the physical aspect.

Which is exactly the opposite of where this relationship started, so I vow to myself to focus strictly on the emotional connection moving forward. But lord, the sex was good and if I'm to be addicted to anything in my life, it's sex with Noah Kneland.

Chapter 36

OLIVIA

Today's going to be my favorite day with Noah yet, I already know it. I can feel it. You know when you wake up in the morning, the sun is shining, but it's not too hot or too cold? Warm enough to leave the window open, because the city is busy but quiet, and it's just perfect today. You can just tell it's going to be a good day.

And I get to spend it with Noah.

I have been going to Fisher Creek a lot lately with Noah's rehab, and Penelope officially moving back in with my parents, so it's just easier for me to go there.

Plus being home has been a secret blessing in disguise, I didn't know I needed. I had no idea how much I truly missed being a hop, skip, and a jump away from my family, especially Liam and Leo. Since they've moved back I have been tasked with emptying my room so they can have it to share. Really, I think it's so Penelope has the opportunity to have some privacy to herself. This divorce has been exceptionally hard on her and she was completely blindsided by it.

I still have trouble to this day believing that Jonathon could be such a shitty person and that Pen was going through this alone.

She was the glue holding the family together as children.

Mom and Dad were both incredibly busy with work, and providing for a family of six that we relied on Penelope for lunches, organizing our rides to and from extracurricular activities, planning play dates, and everything in between. She did what was necessary for the boys and me, and sometimes I can't help but wonder who did what was necessary for her.

Today is the first date Noah and I have had in Milwaukee and I couldn't be more excited.

We have been talking about the books we're reading and recommending books to each other, so I am excited because we are finally doing the bookbinding class at the art center downtown, as well as going to a new Mediterranean restaurant and then I'm going to take him for a walk down by the Milwaukee Riverwalk to get some ice cream as long as the weather continues to cooperate with us.

I woke up extra early today, my internal alarm clock entirely too excited to stay in bed any longer. I basically skip out to the kitchen for a cup of peach green tea to start the day. Caroline and Savannah are sitting around the island, looking half asleep with their cups of coffee, not saying a word.

Clearly, they did not wake up on the same side of the bed as me.

"God, you're chipper this morning" Caroline hisses, putting down her cup and placing both hands on her head as if it's going to explode.

"Sorry, late night?" I ask apologetically.

"The tequila did most of the talking for her last night," Savannah chimes in with a devious smirk on her face and Caroline glares at her as if it's all Savannah's fault she's hungover.

Mason is out of town for his brother's bachelor party so Caroline and Savannah wanted to go out for a night on the town as well. I decided to stay in to be well-rested and ready for today.

I chuckle, shaking my head at Caroline and get back to making my tea. I try to keep it down the best I can knowing how Caroline is after drinking a vat of tequila.

"Why are you so happy this morning?" Savannah asks, keeping the conversation going quietly so as not to disturb the beast next to her.

"Noah's coming down today for our day date in Milwaukee and I'm excited to spend time with him in the city. It's been nice going home every week, but the city is just so special and I want to share that with him," I ramble without even realizing how fast I'm talking.

"It looks like the perfect spring day to be out."

"Yeah, we're meeting at the art center behind the museum, so I'm just going to walk over and enjoy the sunshine. When is Mason coming back? Are you doing anything today?"

"He is jonesing to come home but they still have another night of trouble to get in," Savannah says, looking a little solemn that he isn't back yet. I'm not surprised Mason wants to come home already, he's almost eight years older than his brother, and the children as we call them are wild and immature, children. I wouldn't be surprised if they drag him to the strip club, and are try to jagerbomb everyone. I know Mason loves his brother but half the time says he's too old to handle us girls when we go out and we are almost always home before midnight.

We chat for a bit longer before I decide to head back to my room to get ready for the day. I opt for a mint green corduroy skirt with black tights, booties, and a black long-sleeve bodysuit. The body suit has a square neckline and accentuates my chest in the best way. This outfit feels like the perfect choice because I can add a light jacket if it gets a little chilly, which is entirely possible down by the lake.

When I finish curling my hair, I grab my bag and head back through the house to leave.

As I walk into the open kitchen, and living room, space I'm bombarded with whistles and claps from Caroline and Savannah, who are clearly in favor of my outfit.

I laugh and continue to the door.

"Go get 'em, girl," Savannah calls.

"Don't do anything I wouldn't do," Caroline replies.

"Oh good, there's nothing I can't do today then," I joke back. Caroline's is the type of person who says she'll try anything once but even if she doesn't enjoy it, she'll try it again simply on the grounds that she may like it the second time. "We will see you guys tonight" I yell as I walk through the door and close it behind me.

The art center is three blocks from our house so it's a quick walk over. I arrive with about ten minutes to spare, so I try to sign in but they aren't letting anyone in until five minutes before.

It's a little weird that Noah hasn't arrived yet and that I haven't heard from him. But there are two Buck playoff games this weekend so traffic is definitely heavier.

> **Me: Hey, I'm out front! Can't wait to see you.**

I shoot Noah a text, hoping he sees it.

Two minutes pass, and I've been checking for a reply, but there's nothing.

> **Me: Are you close? They are starting to sign people in.**

I want to go in to get a good spot and pick the best book to re-bind. But I also don't want to go in and be separated from Noah.

Every second that passes where I don't hear back from him feels like an eternity. I decide to call him in case he is driving. After four rings it goes to voicemail, so I decide to leave a message.

"Noah, where are you? They are letting people into the class."

"Miss, it's time to go inside. They are about to start." The nice older lady taps me on the shoulder to make sure I know it's about to start.

"I'm just waiting for my friend," I reply.

"I know, honey, they just don't let people in after the class starts," she replies.

I dial him one more time. This time it doesn't even ring and goes straight to voicemail. My heart breaks a little but I don't leave another message. I'm a lot of things, but desperate and reliant is not one of them.

"I guess he's not coming," I turn to say to the lady, who looks at me with very sad eyes.

"I'm ready, can you show me where the class is?" I finish.

I head into the class, create a beautiful, custom binding for one of my favorite books, and decide one thing for sure: I will never let Noah Kneland play with my heart ever again.

He broke me once shame on him. But to let him in again, shame on me.

I will never make that mistake again.

Chapter 37

NOAH

"What the actual fuck, Kneland?" I hear Cole yell as he comes barrelling into the weight room at the fire station. I put my weights down and stagger my steps to ensure I stay steady for what is about to happen.

Cole is going to kill me, and I'd say I don't deserve it but I missed my date with Ollie on Friday and haven't seen any of the Bennetts since. Hopefully Carter isn't with him, because then I might actually die. We may be adults now but, to this day, Carter is still the most terrifying Bennett there is. There is something about him, his dark demeanor, that keeps me on edge, and doing everything in my power to stay on his good side.

The door to the weight room is already open but judging by the way Cole just ran through the frame he was hoping to slam through it. I stay silent as he approaches and shoves me.

"Why did I just get off the phone with Liv, losing her absolute shit saying you stood her up on your date?" Another shove. Harder this time. A few of the guys put down their equipment to stand by. "I fucking vouched for you, and not even a month into it you do this shit again? What the fuck?"

I finally open my mouth to say something but he shoves me twice as hard as the first two times knocking me backward. This time, the guys jump in and grab Cole's arms before he does it again.

"I deserve that," is all I can bite out at first.

The glare Cole gives me is the equivalent of him taking a butcher knife and stabbing it into my ribcage and twisting.

"There is no excuse for not calling Olivia. I know that I fucked up. But before you beat the hell out of me which I will let you lLet me at least tell you why I missed our date. Please." I feel like I'm begging my best friend to not dump me like a high schooler would.

The guys have let go of Cole's arms and he turns his body so that it's half facing the door out of the weight room and half facing me, indicating to follow.

This is my favorite thing about him, he may be angry, he may want to kill me, but he has always been reasonable, level-headed, and thorough in getting all of the information. I follow him out of the weight room and we settle into his office, where he pours each of us a cup of coffee. He doesn't sit behind his booming oak desk but in the dark red, leather swivel chairs facing the desk. I'm grateful, because otherwise, it's like I'M sitting in Principal Watson's office all over again.

I take a moment to gather myself, sigh, and look down at my coffee before I begin.

"Shit, dude, that is fucked up. How are you?" Cole asks when I finish speaking. He didn't say a word the entire time I spoke, just listened and for that I'm grateful. If he had started asking questions midway through I don't know if I could have finished telling him. I may have gone through years and years of therapy but talking about this has never been easy and I don't suspect it will get any easier now.

"I don't know," I reply. Because I don't know how I am feeling. I have not had time to process it, and I feel shitty about standing up Olivia. I just want to go to her to explain everything and hold her in my arms. "She isn't responding to any of my phone calls or text messages, so I'm going to drive out there to see her, and try to explain," I add.

"She's working today, she just finished lunch and gets off at seven tonight. Go shower, and get out there. She will understand, Noah. Go talk to her, don't stress about the rest of the shift, go take care of yourself," Cole says, and before he even finishes his sentence I'm out the door running to my car.

I know I fucked up. I know I should have called her, I should have let her know what was going on. But there wasn't time, not until it was too late.

She hasn't responded to any of my text messages or calls since Saturday, granted it's only Monday now, but still, after two days I figured she would say something; even if it was just to tell me to fuck off.

It's a super gloomy evening where the sky is full of dark gray clouds, the kind that makes you want to just curl up under a giant blanket and read a book. It almost looks like we're just going to skip summer and fall and head straight back into the winter season where the dark clouds open into a cold snowstorm.

The weather clearly understands that today is going to be a rough day, facing Olivia after accidentally standing her up. One moment there's blue sky, with light fluffy clouds in the air and the next it's full of the dark clouds, making it appear like it is going to start a downpour any second.

It reminds me of the days when we were teenagers and Ollie wanted to spend the day with Cole and I, but we were young and preferred his "annoying" little sister stayed away. She would go from being a sunshiny high schooler, to a literal stormy gremlin and wouldn't talk to us for days.

So, as I pull into the parking spot by her car at work, hoping to catch her before she leaves for home, I hope she'll talk to me.

I back in next to her car, get out, and wait, leaning against my car. I last all of thirty seconds before I start pacing, the anxiety hitting me in every corner of my body.

She'll listen, and understand and everything is going to be fine. I tell myself over and over.

"Noah? Why are you here?" I hear from behind me.

"Ollie," I say, turning around. She's stopped five feet away. I start to move toward her but she takes a step back and puts her hand up indicating for me to stop. She is trying to keep a distance. She doesn't even have to say a word for me to know how hurt she is.

"I'm sorry," I say, looking from her to the ground and back up to her.

"Okay," she says. Okay so still mad. Good to know.

"Ollie" I begin to say before she cuts me off.

"You drove all the way here to tell me that you're sorry. I know you're sorry. You've said it in every text message and voicemail you've left me since Saturday. Has it occurred to you that I don't want to talk to you?" Her words sting, another gut punch. I can see her eyes getting watery, is it from anger? Pain? Sadness?

"Let me explain, Olivia, please," I say, moving closer to her. "I didn't mean to hurt you".

"No, Noah. I don't want to hear your excuses. it's the same damn thing you did in Oklahoma. You don't love me and you never did. I'm done, Noah. I can't go through this again. So leave, go back to Fisher Creek. I don't want to see you. I don't want to talk to you. Do not come to my place of work or my house again."

I freeze. I have no words. She turns away, gets in her car and drives away without looking back. I'm left standing there in the parking lot, mouth dropped, and all alone when I realize there is a tear running down my face.

Everything is not fine. Now I'm driving back to Fisher Creek. Broken. Utterly broken.

Chapter 38

OLIVIA

Driving back to Fisher Creek this weekend feels wrong. There is no light, no excitement...only heartbreak, anger, and fear of running into Noah in town. He hasn't even tried to message or call me since he showed up at my work to apologzie. And I understand I told him I never wanted to see or talk to him again but I thought he'd fight for us this time around.

I thought that because he never stopped loving me, he'd never actually let me go. I guess I was wrong.

It's ungodly warm for a May day in Wisconsin and I think the air conditioning in my car is finally starting to give up on me.

Thankfully, I just pulled off the interstate and only have another hour to cruise down the back roads, so I can roll the windows down. I know my hate for the windows being down on the interstate is irrational and ridiculous, but I absolutely despise the noise the windows make. It's like this never-ending rattle that gets ingrained into my brain and never leaves.

I have my road trip playlist on my aux cord when "Backroad Song by Granger Smith comes on, and I'm instantly overwhelmed with emotion. I feel my eyes welling up with salty water and I have to quickly blink them away. This song sends me back to high school when Noah and I would cruise around in his car singing and dancing to whatever country song we were obsessed with that week.

I think this song obsession lasted a good three weeks before we changed it.

It's such a heartwarming, happy memory but it also makes me realize how much I really miss Noah.

For the last week I've told myself that I'm not allowed to miss him, this was a sign from the universe that we really were not meant to be. I haven't allowed myself to truly process and feel the loss, sadness, and emotion of everything that happened. I have drowned myself in my training even signing up for a marathon in the fall and work, picking up extra hours at the office.

Mason and Savannah cornered me in the kitchen this morning to tell me they're worried about me and that I'm going to burn out hard and fast if I keep going at the pace I am. My response was that I can't burn out if I don't stopped moving, knowing full well how utterly false that is and that they're right.

But truthfully, I'm afraid to stop. I'm afraid that if I stop working or running I will fall back into that deep slump I was in when this happened the first time.

Pulling back into the driveway at my parents' house, it appears that everyone is home. Cole comes out of the house, stops at his truck, and grabs something out of the front seat as I'm getting out of my car about to greet him before going inside. I throw my weekender bag over my shoulder and stand as he walks up to me, but instead of walking up to me, he walks directly past me and into the barn without saying a word.

My jaw hits the ground and I throw my arms up as I turn and watch him go into the barn, before yelling "Hello to you too!"

I have to do a double take to make sure I have the right twin. Cole never ignores me and always is super excited to see me. Carter, on the other hand, sometimes I don't think he cares whether or not I ever come home to visit. But sure enough, the twin who just walked right past me without saying a word, is my five-ten, short, chestnut haired, espresso eyed, firefighter brother.

When I get in the house I see a note on the table from Penelope saying everyone went to Fishy's for lunch and to meet them there once I'm settled. I love that my family chooses to write handwritten notes instead of sending texts like any other normal person. So I throw my stuff on the stairwell and head back out to the car. I can hear music coming from the shop side of the barn and decide that if Cole wanted to go to Fishy's he would have gone when everyone else left.

The drive to the bar is entirely different when there's no snow on the ground and, the leaves are full and everything is green. What would normally be a terrifying drive is now a beautiful spring drive, even if the sun isn't bright. It's a gloomy day but the weather is warm enough that I can have the window partially down to enjoy some fresh air. Or I'm just heated from being mad at my brother for ignoring me.

I will absolutely ask my sister what the fuck his problem is, and if he has copped an attitude all day.

The lake looks extra gloomy when I arrive as if it's raining over the lake but nowhere else. Bec and a few of her friends who I don't recognize are coming out of the bar laughing with one another as I pull up and get out of my car.

"Hey Bec," I call out. She looks over my direction and her expression changes from a laugh to glare with daggers digging deep gouges into my skin. Okay. Yikes. Apparently everyone is mad at me today.

"Hi Olivia" she replies, stone cold and straight faced.

"How have you been?" I ask, trying to be polite but a little shocked. I know Noah and I aren't speaking but that has never hindered my relationship with Bec in the past.

"I've been better and would be even better if I wasn't talking to you."

Well, fuck. Okay. How have I pissed everyone in this town off in the last two weeks? Bec and her friends push past us and continue walking toward their car.

"Oh, and Olivia, I always knew you were selfish, but I never expected you to be downright cruel," she calls from the car before slamming the door and peeling out of the gravel lot, kicking up a huge cloud of dust and sending tiny pebbles all over the place.

I don't even think I've picked my jaw up from the ground in regard to her last comment before I hear the chime of the door at Fishy's and the shuffling of small feet before I have four little hands wrapping around my legs and two bigger hands on my shoulders.

"You saw that entire thing?" I ask, my voice shaking with confusion, anger and even some sadness. Penelope nods, yes and gives me a big side hug before ushering me into the bar.

"Liv, you didn't hear, did you?" she asks as we sit down at the table with my parents and the boys.

I just sit there in silence, looking at them all confused, while they look at me like someone freaking died. Good lord, I know I ended things with Noah, but no one is dead so why is everyone acting so weird?

Mom takes me hands in hers on the table and says, "Olivia, did you talk to Noah about why he didn't make it to Milwaukee?"

I just shake my head, panic starting to race through my entire body. What the fuck happened in the last week?

"Just me what happened. Stop beating around the bush and get to it. You all know I don't handle the unknown well," I snap. "Sorry," I add at the end, trying to take the harshness out of my tone.

Carter comes walking around the corner from where the bathrooms are, and before he even sit down, he says, "Bec was cleaning out the extra room in their house for renovations and she found a box in the closet, with their fathers name on it. She opened it and found numerous letters to him from his lovers."

I pull my hands away from my mother's, and look at Carter, trying to process that I"ve heard him correctly. Lovers? Like, more than one? Their father was cheating before he died? Oh my god, did his mother know? Is she okay?

I begin to spiral when Carter continues. "No, their mother didn't know. And, Liv, I'm on Team Noah for this one. I'm mad at you but you need to know the truth, and clearly everyone else here is going to continue to baby you like the child that you are."

I shudder at the bite behind his statement. I'm literally the baby of the family and they always said I got special treatment and, was able to get away with murder and all of the stereotypical stuff, but I always thought that's just what people say. *Until today.*

My family has always sugar-coated major events in the past when telling me, assumingly to protect my big emotions. Penelope moving, explaining death, when people or animals pass away. And fine, that made sense, when I was ten, but I'm a whole, twenty-eight-year-old adult.

"Thank you, Carter," I respond trying to hide some of my anger.

"Don't. I have zero plans on spending time with you until you figure your shit out," he retorts as he gets up to leave. My parents' mouths hang open, looking like deer stuck in the headlights at how Carter's speaking to me. Carter and I fight, and are likely the meanest to each other, but it's typically in good fun. However, today there's no sarcasm in his voice, it's just plain mean.

"Honey," Mom starts before I cut her off.

"No Mom, Carter is right, all of you have always sugar-coated everything. And in reality there is no part of life that is sugar coated. I'm an adult, working as a physical therapist for some of the most demanding jobs, in the biggest city in the state. I understand that life is hard out there, that it's not fair, and heartbreak is part of that. I also know that I have a lot of emotions, and they are big and loud and deep. But I'm damn proud to be able to feel and love as large as I do, even if it hurts in the long run," I say, standing up from the table, needing some air and space to figure out what exactly is going on with Noah and his family.

And unfortunately my brothers are probably the best place to start.

Chapter 39

OLIVIA

After two hours spent in the barn with Cole, and eventually Carter, I have the full picture. And, man, do I feel like a piece of shit. I tried to text Noah on my way home from Fishy's, thinking maybe I could bypass his fan club and go right to him, but he didn't answer. I even tried to call, and was sent to voicemail. He is taking my demands about never speaking again way more seriously than I need at this moment.

Once I finally convinced Cole to talk to me, I learned that Bec found the letters, and was reading them in the breakfast nook, tears streaming down her face when their mother walked in. Bec never heard her coming up the driveway, or even into the house. Since Archie is now living with Noah at his house, he couldn't have even alerted her.

Their mom waltzed right up to Bec, asked what she was reading, grabbed a letter and the first line she read was, *Graham, you have promised to leave your wife and wretched children for almost a year now, I'm starting to believe I'm the fool for believing our love was real.* And that is when everything went to literal shit.

Noah was working a shift at the fire station, but it was a relatively quiet night so they were in the gym getting some additional training in when Bec came flying into the gym out of breath with some of the rest of the crew behind her. Through broken statements, Bec told them what happened and that their mom was on an angry rampage, ready to murder the women who wrote the letter. Who, all too, conveniently lived along the far side of the lake.

I'm glad she went the angry route as opposed to the catatonic one that happened when Mr. Kneland passed away. In reality, I'm angry for her and I want to jump right on the train behind Mrs. Kneland and rock someone's world. This entire situation would be nearly impossible for any of them to understand or even process in such a short amount of time. I can't imagine if Noah has to become a caretaker again.

Noah was able to get to the house before she absolutely lost everything and talked her down from the murderous rage ledge, but in the process Noah left his phone at the station where it later died. They then spent the next three days removing anything related to their father from the house and burned most of it. They experienced a mix of anger, sadness, and confusion and it wasn't until he went back to the firehouse he realized he didn't have his phone. But also when he saw my missed calls, and voicemail.

Noah did exactly what he's always done best, dropped everything and showed up for the people he loves in a crisis. And what had I done? I had been so caught up in my own thoughts and feelings of reliving the past that I wasn't even willing to hear him out. What does that make me? Certainly not a good friend, or a girlfriend.

I'm not sure where Noah and I stand but one thing is for sure.

I owe him an apology and it's going to be a big one.

I just may need a little bit of help to pull it off.

Chapter 40

Noah

"Come on, bro, you have to go" Cole pleads with me trying to convince me to go to Fishy's for drinks with the guys from work.

"I don't want to deal with people today," I say, which isn't a lie, but in reality, I haven't been to Fishy's in the last two weeks because it brings up too many memories of Ollie, and I don't want to make a stupid decision.

It's been two weeks since I drove out to Milwaukee to explain everything, and she told me she didn't want to see or talk to me again. It may kill me to do so but I'm going to do everything in my power to respect her wishes.

Cole looks at me with a disappointed, loving face before saying "You haven't been out with us in weeks, you can't hide in your house wallowing forever.

"I'm not wallowing." I retort. He's right, I'm absolutely wallowing. I haven't worked on the house in over two weeks. When I'm done at work I either run until I can't stand or go to bed and don't move until I have to get up for work the next day.

Cole just looks at me knowingly.

"Okay, okay, I'll go. But only for an hour and only 'cause the whole crew is going, so I know if I don't show my face I'll never hear the end of it," I finally say.

Cole offers to drive us to Fishy's which is only because he is obsessed with his "new" beat-up red pickup truck. It was his grandfather's, who was recently told he wasn't able to drive anymore so they fixed it up together and then Cole bought it.

I've always been envious of the Bennett children's relationships with their grandparents. Cole and his grandfather hang out regularly sometimes, he even brings him to the station to hang out with us, and we play cards. They tell each other everything. That was the same relationship Ollie had with her grandmother before she passed. Inseparable. Endless love. Bec and I have never really had a relationship with our grandparents.

Once my dad passed, his parents moved out of Wisconsin to Arizona to get away from the cold. Knowing what I know now, I personally think my grandparents knew my father was a cheating piece of shit and didn't want to have to face the trauma he caused within our family. Which makes them just as bad, if not worse.

The sun is high overhead and it's one of those days where you can tell it's just going to be a beautiful, hot day. There isn't a single cloud in the sky and the sky is this pale baby blue that you would envision in a coastal house.

"Damn, there are a lot of people at Fishy's today," I say as we pull into the large gravel parking lot overlooking the lake and the park.

"It's the start of the season, so not entirely surprising," Cole says, getting out of his truck after checking his phone quickly.

The door dings as usual when opened, and I instantly stop in my tracks. There, on the opposite side of the bar stands Ollie, Caroline, Mason, and Savannah, all laughing and drinking. I stand still as they all cheer and take a shot of what looks like whiskey.

I turn to walk back out the door when Bec waves obnoxiously from a table with Cole and a few of the guys from the department. If there's anything I hate more than hurting Ollie, it's disappointing and upsetting my sister. I shake my head, look towards the floor, and walk directly to the table.

"What the fuck?" I murmur to Cole, who hands me a beer and a shot of Jameson.

"Savannah and Caroline have never been to the lake and she wanted to show them, I didn't think they were going to be here," Cole responds innocently.

"Fuck them, Noah. We are on the opposite side of the bar, and they didn't even turn when you walked in the bar. You deserve to go out and have fun too," Bec says, slamming the remainder of her drink. If nothing else my sister will always have my back, I swear for a five-foot-one, one-hundred-thirty-pound woman, she isn't one to mess with. She actually kind of reminds me personality-wise of Caroline from that night out at the Pub Down the Street.

"One drink," I say, taking a sip of my hazy beer and watching their small group out of the corner of my eye.

It's karaoke night and I have listened to Caroline and half the department try their hands at singing, Cole included. But I can't seem to pull my eyes from Ollie, her perfect ass and hips fill the soft bell-bottom jeans and the way her wavy chestnut hair frames her face. Her neutral pink lip gloss shimmering on her lips, and I know it's time to leave before I make a fool out of myself.

I slam the Jameson shot in front of me, salute the boys, and stand to walk out the door. I open the door, hear the little jingle, and then hear the music change for the next karaoke singer.

It still feels like our first night together

The voice stops me dead in my tracks, and I turn to confirm what my brain is telling me. Ollie is singing karaoke. She's standing at the end of the platform, staring at me, voice shaking, and tears streaking down her face.

I close the door behind me and continue to watch Ollie sing, oblivious to the cheers for her around me. She steps down off the stage and starts walking toward me.

Part of me wants to just turn away and leave, but seeing her standing up there, being this vulnerable, has my feet nailed to the floor.

The bar erupts with cheers when the song ends, and we're standing inches away from each other. I can't help but smile as Ollie looks at me, tears filling her eyes from embarrassment. She's never liked the spotlight, and that was completely out of her element and comfort zone.

"That was *High School Musical* type shit" I say, crossing my arms in front of my chest to keep myself from touching her. She looks absolutely beautiful tonight, but I have to remember she told me she never wants to hear from me again. I have to respect that. She laughs through the tears, and everyone around us goes back to drinking and chatting, as if nothing even happened.

"You've never even seen *High School Musical*," she says, trying to sound menacing but she's too full of emotion for it to come across accurately.

"No, but that is what I imagine it to look like," Even if we can never move past what happened, I'm going to live in this moment here forever.

"There is one more thing I want to show you," Olivia says, placing her hands on my forearms, stepping closer before walking past me, to lead us outside.

"Ollie..."

"Noah, I owe you an apology and not just a small I'm sorry a big true apology but before we get there I have to show you something."

"Where are we going?" I ask hesitantly as she gets in her car.

"Do you trust me, Noah?" she says half smirking, hand shaking as she places it on the steering wheel, clearly nervous and trying to steady it.

"I have always trusted you," I whisper.

We drive downtown and park in the angled parking outside the empty dance studio where Bec used to dance. Unfortunately, the studio closed a few years ago because there weren't enough dancers anymore and it's been empty ever since. The space is perfect, centrally located, with huge windows in the front, a large open space on one side, and some smaller rooms on the other side in the back.

Then I see it the new white and green sign outside the dance studio, and the big red ribbon across the doorway.

"What is this?" I ask, confused.

"Welcome to Bennett Rehabilitation & Performance," she says, smiling ear to ear while her, cheeks start turning red, probably with nervousness and anxiety.

I just stand next to Ollie, confused looking at the building.

"You bought a building in Fisher Creek?" I ask, trying to decipher what's happening. "Ollie, you live in Milwaukee."

"Not anymore," she replies. "I bought this building and am opening a practice here in Fisher Creek. After your accident, I realized there's a huge need for physical therapy and performance-based care here. I can fix that. Plus, I get to be closer to you." she continues, saying the last part quieter.

"Ollie" I start, but she cuts me off.

"Wait, let me finish, please, before I lose my nerve and don't say any of this at all." She's holding and twisting her hands in front of me, trying to keep herself occupied. "I was wrong. I know that now, and I'm so incredibly sorry for what I said to you and that I wasn't there for you when you needed me the most. Truthfully, loving you is the scariest thing in my life and I'm terrified of being hurt again. I didn't know at the moment that shutting you out to protect myself would actually hurt both of us more than ever." She's fighting back the second tsunami of emotion about to crash over her, but I stay quiet to let her finish. Seeing her this upset is a punch to the gut, and I don't even need to hear her finish to know I want her in my arms forever. "I should have listened to you and communicated better about how I was feeling and taken into consideration that there are other factors in life that may play a part in your actions. It was childish and immature, and I'm sorry, Noah," she finishes while looking at her hands, and then drops them to her sides and looks up at me.

"I forgive you, Ollie, but I cannot let you give up Milwaukee to be closer to me," I add because I will never let her give up her dreams and aspirations for me. Or for anyone, for that matter.

"Dreams change, Noah," she says, and my heart instantly melts into a giant puddle. "Opening this practice in Fisher Creek is my dream. It allows me to do what I love while being closer to and with the people who mean the most to me. I'm not giving up my dream for you. I'm striving to live my dream with you. I may not know what the future looks like for us but I know that I want you in it."

"I love you, Olivia Bennett," I say as I grab her hips and pull her body close to mine, kissing her lips.

"I love you, Noah Kneland." She kisses me back.

Epilogue – 3 years later

OLIVIA

They say time flies when you're having fun, and I always thought that to be a bit of a cliche until I fell back in love with my best friend. Love is supposed to be messy, with ups, downs and all arounds but as long as you fall deeper in love with your person each day, you're doing it right.

I will remember each of those critical falling moments, where you are so invested in someone that your stomach hurts, that you even remember what your life was before those moments.

I have had exactly four of those moments with Noah.

1. The first day of our last harvest season together, when he wrapped his arm around me

2. Signing karaoke at Fishy's

3. Walking down the aisle on our wedding day last year

4. Finding out we're pregnant

Until today, the last moment has always been my favorite. *Standing at the top of the aisle looking down to every important person in my life, and seeing Noah standing there, tears welling in his eyes.*

In that moment, as I stands at the edge of the aisle, it's like the world narrows to a single point of focus, Noah. My heart pounds so hard in my chest that I swear everyone around me can hear it. But not with nerves, a more overwhelming emotion: love, joy, a little disbelief that it's finally here. I know there are many people here, perks of living in a small town, everyone is excited for a wedding, and everyone actually shows up too. But as I begin my descent down the aisle their faces become unrecognizable, their presence distant, fading into the background. My breath catches when we lock eyes, because in that instant, nothing else matters. It's not the dress, not the guests, not even the ceremony, food or even the journey we took to get here. just us silently screaming, "I choose you. I love you."

Which is exactly what I plan to do, choose Noah each day knowing he will be there to catch me through it all. But today is different, we are no longer just choosing each other, we are choosing our child too and somehow I think today is going to become my favorite day of falling in love with my husband.

Walking out our giant sliding glass door onto the newly built wooden deck that overlooks our property to see all of our favorite people in the yard, together celebrating has me realizing that this is the ultimate dream.

Mason jumps off the steps of the deck roaring as he plays Dinosaurs and Dragons with my nephews. My mom and Noah's mom are standing over the gift table, making a list of everyone who brought gifts today so that thank-you cards can go out later. Carter and Bec are sitting on the outdoor sectional with beers in hand, chatting quietly but also looking uninterested in the party which is on par. The guys from the fire department are all standing with Noah and Cole around the grill, chatting and laughing. They really have been a godsend since moving back home, creating another sense of home and family for this move and transition. Caroline and Savannah come into the picture through the sliding glass door with a beautiful cake indicating that it's almost time for the party to start.

I feel a hand on my shoulder and turn to see Penelope standing next to me, smiling ear to ear. Her divorce has been official for just over two years and it's a breath of fresh air to see her out and about, not only out and about, but smiling as well. This time hasn't been an easy transition for anyone but I wouldn't want anyone else standing next to me.

"I'm really glad you are here today, Pen," I say, turning to give her a hug.

"You know I wouldn't miss your baby shower or gender reveal party. However, I secretly hope it's a girl because we have enough crazy little boys around here to last us a lifetime," she responds, pulling me in close. "You are creating the most beautiful life, Liv, and I couldn't be more proud of you."

"These damn hormones really are the damn worst," I say, laughing at her and she laughs back at me in agreement.

When moving home, my biggest fear was losing my relationship with my Milwaukee friends and family, but exactly the opposite happened. When they say distance makes the heart grow fonder I didn't think it corresponded to friendships as well, but they have only grown in amazing ways. Caroline just moved to Fisher Creek to escape the city after feeling overwhelmed by fast-paced city life, and has since taken her auntie role, very seriously.

Noah had kept a distance from the guys at the station, afraid to develop a relationship with any of them due to the fear of it being ripped away in the blink of an eye. Trauma does funny things to people, and watching someone work through all of their trauma, personal, professional, and familial to grow and achieve the happiness they deserve is amazing. Actually doing the work and experiencing the ups and downs of working through trauma together alongside the man you love is an entirely different game, one I will forever be grateful for.

Noah has been able to build relationships and friendships through work that he never would have been able to do before limiting our ability to be where we are today.

"Hi, everyone!" Caroline shouts with a loud clap of her hands. Everyone silences and turns to look at her standing on a small bench so everyone can see her. "I want to thank you all for being here to celebrate Liv and Noah's little bundle of joy. We didn't tell anyone that today is actually a dual party for both a baby shower and a gender reveal. So, *surprise,* we are about to get to the fun part of the night, finding out if this bundle is a boy or girl!" She turns to each of us, motioning for both of us to come over to the small bar top table holding a cake.

The cake is absolutely beautiful, made by Bec, who recently announced she'd like to open a bakery. It's a cranberry lemon cake with cream cheese frosting, and of course the middle layer has either blue or pink frosting in it to indicate what our little munchkin is. I know everyone thinks we're having a baby girl, but I secretly want it to be a boy. I can envision Noah and our son, in the yard kicking a soccer ball back and forth, or standing on the dock by the pond at the back of the house fishing together.

We gather around the cake, Noah wrapping his arm around my waist and pulling me close. He turns to plant a kiss on the top of what used to be freshly curled hair but the random burst of humidity, paired with the weight and explosive hormones had other thoughts.

"Ready?" he whispers, almost shaking with excitement. When I told him I was pregnant, I burst into tears, not happy tears, terrified tears while he put his hands over his mouth, did a little happy hop, and then wrapped me in the most secure hug of all time telling me that everything's going to be okay. And he was right.

All our family and friends are around us looking at us with eyes wide and, ear-to-ear smiles, some silent happy tears sneaking down their faces, waiting for us to cut the cake. We decided today to have a cake just for us and cupcakes for everyone else. Bec and Caroline, might be the only two people to know the gender, but I think they are the most excited to share this moment with us.

We look at each other, then I close my eyes and jab the cake on the count of three. Everyone around us erupts with cheers, and I hear my mom gasp and start crying before we even open our eyes. I'm overwhelmed with emotion hearing everyone around us but am too anxious to actually open my eyes and find out. I don't care what gender our baby is, they are going to be loved no matter what.

"Ollie, open your eyes," Noah whispers, and I can feel the endless happiness coming through his words as he squeezes me close.

I open my eyes and look up at him for a split second before glancing at the cake, blue. I gasp, dropping my glass and bringing my hands up to my mouth as the tsunami of tears stream down my face.

"You're going to be the best boy mom," Noah whispers into my hair before planting the biggest kiss on the top of my head.

Bonus Epilogue – 3 years later

NOAH

I *have sat down to write this at least 50 times in the last year or so but never really felt ready. Until about 3 months ago when I walked into our bedroom and saw Ollie sitting on the edge of the bench, head in her hands, shaking.*

That day replays in my mind, like a movie constantly streaming. I rushed in there and dropped to one knee in front of her, hands on her forearms.

"What happened babe?"

She doesn't answer me, but her body continues to tremble. And then I see it. The white stick with the little blue cross in the middle.

"Oh, Ollie." I take her from the bench and into my lap. "It's okay, we will figure everything out."

"What about my practice? We aren't ready for children yet."

"We will figure it out. This is a good thing, you're going to be an amazing mom."

We sit there in the bedroom, Ollie wrapped in my arms like a tortilla wraps around a burrito in silence for another few minutes. Secretly I'm ecstatic about this news. Knowing we decided to wait until everything felt more stable and consistent but I think this is the best news for us.

Except all I wanted to do was call you, to tell you the news to thank you for getting me here. And fuck man. This is hard. I want to say that I am over your death, that I have come to terms with losing you but I don't think you ever come to terms with losing your best friend.

But I thought you should know.

I came home. I found Ollie. I went to therapy. I found a friendship with Cole again.

It wasn't easy. She wasn't willing to give me a chance immediately, she was shy and sheltered, with walls up protecting her heart. Her heart that I tore out of her chest. That I broke, and was asking for a chance to peel off the bandaids and to show her that the love we shared all those years ago still exists. That I loved her everyday for those ten years. That I will continue to love her everyday.

When I thought I finally broke a piece of the wall down, when we had a chance to live the life we both deserved we found out that Dad was cheating on Mom, and everything spiraled out of control.

And you weren't here.

Cole and I got into a fight.

You still weren't here.

And I wondered if you really had any idea what you were talking about in your letter. Did I deserve this torture for not saving you, for hurting Ollie?

But she came back. She told me she loved me, and she always would. She moved back to Fisher Creek and man you would love her. She is strong, and independent but also passionate and fierce. She is selfless in caring for me, her family and this entire community. You'd be two peas in a pod, tearing this town apart and ganging up on me with all of your jokes.

Now we are going to be a family. I am going to have a child, to take care of and love with me entire heart, and I am terrified but excited. I know this is going to be hard. But everything in life that is worth it is hard.

I know you said, you know what it's like to be unhappy and alone. To be unloved by those who you want to love you unconditionally. But I thought you should know, Schmidty, you are loved. I love you. I thank God, everyday for giving me a friend like you to push me to do the hard things. Because I never would have come home. I never would have reached out to Ollie and I never would have found this amazing life that I continue to cherish day in and day out.

Thank you Jarred, for being my friend, for everything.

I just thought you'd like to know that I am happy, and I did everything.

"Noah, are you ready to go?" I hear, coming from down the hallway. We have finally finished the renovations of the house and I know she is in the soon to be nursey, planning how we are to going decorate it.

"Almost." I cap my pen, wipe the single, silent tear that is creeping slowly down by face and fold the paper into perfect thirds before standing and walking over to the dark brown wooden built in bookshelves on the far side of the office.

"We can't be late for this appointment," she calls again.

Pulling out a small box, placing it on the desk I open it and look inside. The letter and dog tags sit perfectly inside. Placing the new letter inside, I smile to myself knowing that Jarred would be happy.

He thrived off making everyone around him happy, even sacrificing his own to achieve that.

After returning the box to its designated spot on the shelf next to a half blurry photo of us leaving Fishy's one night, I turn and see Ollie standing in the doorway, leaning against the doorframe with on hand on her tiny round belly, that is just starting to show, with a beautiful smirk on her face.

"He'd be proud of you and happy to see this," she says, waving me closer to her.

"I know," I say, pulling her close and planting a kiss on her forehead.

Acknowledgements

Wow, guys, we did it. I am actually so baffled and amazed that we made it to the end and release of this book. The support and love I have had throughout has been beyond amazing.

To Macayla and Leslie thank you for the zoom calls, the texts, and knocking me off my ledge when things get tough.

Cause if you've written a book before, you know that there are a lot of tough moments.

Y'all are the greatest hype team there is.

Writing a book is a little like falling in love—messy, thrilling, full of plot twists, and only made possible by the people who stick with you through the chaos.

To my editor, Caroline, thank you for seeing the potential in this story and all of my stories. I appreciate your hard work, time and commitment to not only myself but all of the other authors you work with. You are truly one of the kindest people I have met and have helped me in so many ways as I navigate this journey.

To my beta readers, thank you for reading early drafts, the unhinged comments, and the authentic reading reactions. I live for them and appreciate you getting me through this.

To my friends and family: thanks for pretending not to notice when I disappeared into fictional worlds and for loving me even when I spoke in plot points.

To every reader who picked up this book and gave these characters a chance, you are the heartbeat behind why I write. I hope this book made you smile, laugh, cry and fall in love with Jarred and Julie.

And finally, to love itself, it is messy, hard, but worth the risk.

Thank you, thank you, thank you.

I aprpeaciate you all.

About the author

Sierra Zinke is a romantic at heart who has the biggest soft spot for a good love story. She writes romance full of love, heat and emotion. Her books are full of big feelings, and feel like real life.

A northern girl at heart currently falling in love with the south as she lives in North Carolina with her other half and their two pups.

When she is not busy writing, she is a practicing chiropractor in North Carolina, striving to help people continue their favorite activities. Otherwise she truly loves reading, sports, and trying new restaurants.

You can check out her books at www.zinkewrites.com and say hi on social media @zinkewrites!!!

Also by

9 798999 183093 5